PRAISE

A touching reflection on family, motherhood, identity, and forgiveness that may encourage readers to do more work on their own close relationships. The prose is stylishly straightforward, which not only makes the book a quick and easy read, but also lends the characters a raw simplicity that makes it hard not to root for a happy ending.

— SELF-PUBLISHING REVIEW

Shelley's near rhapsodic prose allows her stories to bloom. Readers completing this novel will likely be eager for the next installment!

— GRADY HARP, HALL OF FAME TOP 100 AMAZON REVIEWER

Shelley Kassian is a talented author with a lot of potentials when it comes to storytelling.

— KERRIE, VINE VOICE AMAZON REVIEWER

A Sea for Summer was easy reading—perfect for sitting on the dock at my cottage with a cocktail in hand. The beautiful scenery, romance, and just the right amount of conflict comprised the book, and it was the escape I was craving.

— STEPHANIE ELIZABETH, ONLINE BOOK CLUB

This really was a nice change in pace for me and as there are other books that are to follow this one, I look forward to picking up the next ones and seeing what becomes of the other characters mentioned within this story. One I would reread.

— MARALLE TALLEY, SKYBOOKCHAT

Kassian's measured prose is pitch-perfect—good writing sustains, but 'great' writing elevates, and at the end of the day, regardless of where you fall on the romance genre, this book is a cut above.

— JAMES W, VINE VOICE AMAZON REVIEWER

Well-written and captivating! A fascinating journey of second chances.

— KINDLE READER

A Sea for Summer

Shelley Kassian

ALSO BY SHELLEY KASSIAN

Contemporary Romance

Places in the Heart:

A Mountain Leads Home, Book 2

The Thurston Hotel:

A Lasting Harmony, Book 5

The Women of Stampede:

The Half Mile of Baby Blue, Book 2

Historical Romance

A Sacrifice for Love

A Heart across the Ocean

A Gentleman for Christmas

Shelley Kassian writing as Abby Lane

Dark Fantasy

A Reign of Blood and Magic:

The Scarlett Mark, Book 1

The Ebony Queen, Book 2

The Immortal Blood, Book 3

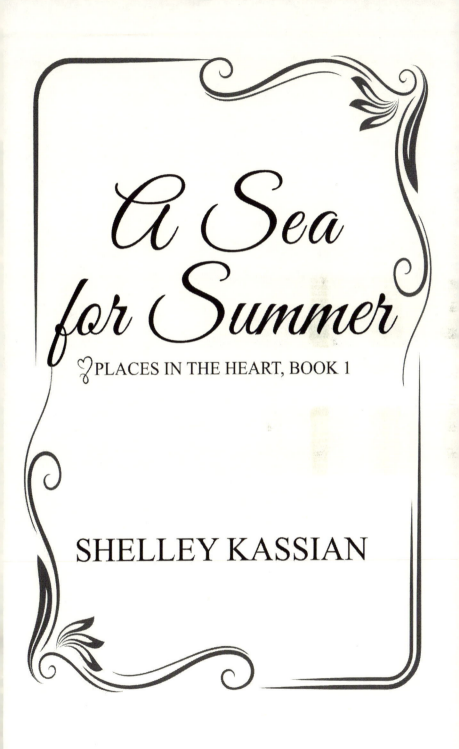

A Sea for Summer

♡ PLACES IN THE HEART, BOOK 1

SHELLEY KASSIAN

Published 2021 by Shelley Kassian
(shelleykassian.com)

ISBN: 978-1-7770699-4-0 (Print Edition)
ISBN: 978-1-7770699-5-7 (Digital Edition)

Design and cover art by 100 Covers
Copyediting by Ted Williams

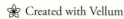 Created with Vellum

DEDICATION

This novel is dedicated to:
Katie O'Connor;
Brenda Sinclair;
S.L. Dickson.

ACKNOWLEDGMENTS

I'm grateful to my husband and family for supporting and inspiring my writing career. Especially my daughter Alicia, who began her own journey as a school and applied child psychologist during the writing of this novel. I called on her advice many times while writing *A Sea for Summer*. She offered character insights that improved the story. One song suggestion inspired much thought: *Not Today* by Imagine Dragons. When I was stuck, I listened to this song, over and over again…

Much thanks to Katie O'Connor for beta-reading this book and suggesting I deepen emotion in key places.

Credit to Ted Williams for copyediting the manuscript. In the wedding scene, he asked me an all-important question: "Why always is it 'you may kiss the bride' and not… 'you may kiss your husband?'"

Much thanks to 100 Covers for my fantastic cover, featuring Peter and Claire gazing lovingly at the sunset.

And finally, thanks to my amazing readers for supporting me by buying this book! I couldn't do this work without you.

CHAPTER ONE

"*Claire…we can't live like this anymore. It's not enough to share space in a house where two people barely meet. We're like strangers, two ships in the night coping with sorrow instead of joy. I don't want to drown in our personal storm. I want to thrive. Something needs to change; we need to change…*"

Claire knew Peter was right. She admitted for the first time that their marriage was in trouble. What could she do about it? When would the pain end? They didn't share space together anymore. When they were in the same room, they hardly spoke two words. Neglect and a lack of communication propelled them toward separation.

Two hearts were broken. How could she mend the break?

Peter had made a valid point; change was necessary to rebuild their marriage. Yet they were so damaged, where should they begin? Where should she begin? What was her starring role in this drama?

Claire didn't know if the problems could be fixed. Peter's

position was clear. His criticism had led to brooding thoughts while preparing the day's assortment of bakery items: pies, bread, and a variety of pastries for the family-owned bakery. The work had begun hours ago. She filled a pan with pastry dough and as she flattened the crust into place, crimping the dough around the edges, rougher than usual, Claire questioned if her marriage had taken its last breath.

Had her bond to Peter Douglas deflated like lost air in a balloon?

In Claire's opinion, one issue was glaringly apparent, her happiness. No different than Peter, she didn't want to face constant turmoil either. They were too volatile. If their voices weren't raised in anger, they were weeping in silence. She missed their laughter, their playful chemistry, the way they used to hold hands. Claire wanted this and more back. How could she get it back?

The bell chimed at the front entrance, announcing her mother's arrival to assist in the day's work. Mary strolled into the back workroom, wearing a broad smile.

"Good morning, how's my girl today?"

Claire blew a wayward strand of hair away from her eyes while reaching for the next pie plate. What should she say? In silence, she watched her mother place her purse on the countertop. She wore familiar clothing: a dusty blue shirt, polyester pants, and a cheerful smile. Her mother held a positive view of the future. Claire wished she shared her mother's optimism as nothing about this Monday morning brightened her spirits.

"I'd rather not say."

"That bad?" Mary asked, her eyebrows rising as he reached for an apron. "Trouble at home again?"

Claire perused her mother's sympathetic expression, swallowing. Her finger tore through the piecrust. *Damn.* The agitation…tears were building behind her eyes and threatening to escape. She should talk to someone about her marriage rather than bottling up her grief. Hiding the truth from her mother had never been an effective solution.

Happiness dimmed to concern. "How bad is it this time?"

"Terrible," Claire said, her lower lip quivering. "We're not talking. Peter didn't come home last night."

"Look, Claire, I know you're a strong woman, preferring to handle situations on your own, but if I can help…"

"There's nothing you can do. Nothing you can say to make the situation better."

Mary grasped an apron, staring at her seriously, soon tying the straps into place. "Peter is a strong-willed bear. But *you* don't like taking advice at the best of times. Maybe my two cubs should consider counselling."

Claire shook her head. The mention of the word 'bear' had her thinking about Peter's ample chest and strong muscular arms that used to embrace her. In her mind, nothing was better than being held in his arms. Emotional, she tossed more pastry dough onto the counter and punched it down, perhaps a little too hard, then began rolling the crust. "I don't have time for relationship negotiations. Neither does Peter."

Mary grasped her hand, preventing further movement. "Make time. A marriage is an investment; you need to give yours more attention. Stop ignoring the problem. When will either of you make an effort, when it's too late?"

"You're not being helpful."

"Look...a mother supports her children, even when they're adults. Above all, my daughter comes first, but Peter is a part of my life, too. Neither of you can address the issues by hoping they'll go away."

Claire didn't know what to say to her mom any different than she knew what to say to Peter. Though her mother made a valid point.

Mary drew closer to her. "I know the situation is complicated. Peter needs to accept his part in the marriage troubles as well. Look, your father and I have been married for, well...forever." Mom shook her head, giving her a slight smile. "Men are difficult to live with on the best of days. I support my daughter, first and foremost, but relationships are never one-sided."

"Your logic makes sense." Knowing her mother grasped the situation didn't make her feel better.

Mary sighed. "Look, you're both my children and I love both of you dearly. I accepted Peter the first time you brought him into the bakery. I acknowledged him as my son the day you said your vows. Years later, two strong adults should address the issues in their marriage before it's too late."

Claire frowned, irritated they were having this discussion. "Mom, I know you mean well, but it's too late to see a counsellor." Emotion compromised her breathing and glistened in her eyes, but she had to disclose the truth. "I think there's someone else."

"Another woman?" Mary asked, her face whitening while pondering the disclosure. "Are you sure?"

Claire rolled the dough, too rough and too fast. "He comes home late at night, thinking I'm asleep, but I've been lying in bed for hours, worrying and waiting." Claire brushed away a tear. "The backdoor banging alerts me someone is home. He enters the bedroom and gathers his pajamas, then retreats to another bedroom and drifts off to sleep. Why won't he sleep with me? Why won't he hold me, hug me? What do I need to do? Where is my husband and who is he visiting late at night?"

Her mother sighed, tapping her fingers on the counter. "Do you still love him?"

Claire swallowed, her emotions raw. "No matter what happens, I'll always love him; I can't sleep for worry about where he is and when he's coming home. I need him. I don't know how to fix us. He's part of me and I don't want to lose him."

"If you love Peter," her mom said firmly, "try not to let doubt enter your mind. It will eat away at your insides; poison you and make the situation worse. You know where your husband sits late at night. At his desk inside his office."

"If that's true, he's not there alone."

Her mother sighed, giving her a surprised look. She moved to the fridge, opened the door, then pulled prepared fruit from inside and placed it on the countertop. "You seem clear on your suspicions. I'm afraid to ask, is there something you're not telling me?"

Claire took a deep breath and released a long, weary sigh.

"I drove by his office the other night. There were two cars parked in the lot."

"Is that so."

"Yes, and I have reason to doubt him." Claire closed her eyes, willing herself not to break down, yet an elusive truth had left her unsure of what she had seen. She stepped away from her mom, offering a view of her back, so her emotion could be somewhat hidden. One night, she'd driven to Peter's office and parked near the building to learn if the boss and his employee's working relationship had grown into something more. "In the early hours of morning, it doesn't seem right that a boss shares a laugh with his office manager, grinning like a fool, when he should be at home with his wife."

"I agree with you, in that some boundaries might be stretching. But building a relationship with Lori when he has you, well...cheating doesn't seem likely to me."

"Doesn't it?" Claire said, a little too loudly, facing her mom. "Shouldn't my husband be at home with me?"

"Of course, he should. You're his number one squeeze. I'm just saying, there's two sides to every conflict. Rather than believing the worst, you should talk to Peter. But in terms of working hours, the two of you have conflicting schedules. Peter probably thinks similarly when you leave the house at five a.m., leaving him alone while you address the bakery's needs."

"What choice do I have? I can't abandon my job; the bakery demands attention. We need to bring back our customers. Our pies were the taste of the town."

Her mother frowned. "Life has its cycles, but this business won't survive if we burn ourselves out." Mary stared at her in a meaningful way. "I can help. We can fix this. We can make changes to the bakery and give Peter and you more time together. Nora Jones has been looking for a job. She's forceful with her ideas, but the bakery needs bold concepts."

"Maybe."

Claire had been so upset the night before, she'd come to the bakery after leaving Peter's office to prepare today's pie fillings. She hadn't been home yet. Why should she bother? Peter wouldn't be in their bed anyway.

Her mother filled the completed pie shells with peach filling while seeming to reflect on the ingredients, delicately placing peaches in the shell while shaking her head.

"It takes work to have a successful business. My children work diligently at two separate places. One leaves too early in the morning and the other comes home too late at night. I wish I had wise words or practical solutions that could bring you back together."

"I know you mean well, Mom, but there's nothing you can do. Maybe it's best to keep our discussion on the pies."

"We're having a peachy day. It's the perfect flavor for summer, especially with a dollop of vanilla ice cream. But I thought we'd make a key lime pie. Refreshing and delicious during the summer months," her mom said, giving her an uneasy smile.

"Mom, please stop."

"It's Peter's favorite. Maybe you could take it to him. A goodwill offering."

Claire thrust an empty pie plate away, clutching her aching head. She massaged her temples. "I can't talk about this anymore."

"Of course, you're upset." Her mom took control of the situation like some mothers did. "Turn the oven on. Let's focus on our work; finish the pies, get them in the oven and bake them before our first customer arrives."

"The few customers we have."

Claire didn't feel like talking, so held the pain and grief inside. Mother and daughter worked in companionable silence, not speaking, until the last pie cooled off on the counter.

CHAPTER TWO

Claire's mother nudged her elbow. "Let's talk about something happier. Isn't it almost time for the yearly retreat?"

"Yes." Claire mulled over the event, wondering if she should attend. "It's set for the last weekend in May. Everyone's going except Portia."

"I suppose Anne's busy with her lavender farm."

"She's opening a gardening store soon, complete with plants, gifts, and a café. She'll sell candles, hand cream, bath salts and herbal tea. The main ingredients were grown on her farm."

"That's impressive. She's brought new life to her grandparents' farm. They'd be proud of her."

"I'm glad you think so, as I thought we could support her by carrying some of the products at the bakery."

"That's a great idea. It never hurts to diversify. Anne made a wise decision when she chose to grow lavender, but a woman's success can create complications." Mary gave Claire a contemplative look. "If you're not careful, you'll end up like your friend."

"What, divorced? Mom, that's not fair. The two situations are vastly different. Anne's husband left her for a younger woman."

"He's a good-for-nothing louse," her mother said frankly. "She's better off without him."

Claire shrugged. "Strong words, even for you. Though it doesn't matter one way or the other. They're long past over."

"I suppose Laina will be able to attend," Mary said, her tone probing, "given she has a pause in her acting career."

"If you're referring to the headlines in the newspapers and the media reporting about a difficult actress, Laina had good reasons to rebel against the film's producer and the movie contract."

"I heard the love scene cut into the deal."

"A sex scene, actually," Claire said, making a face. "Laina's always wanted to meet her soulmate, but *not* with her chest exposed in the company of castmates, who for all intents and purposes, are strangers. She's saving herself for a real partner. Fake intimacy is not what she intended when she signed up for this movie role."

"I thought the actor playing the lead had a sexy body." Her mom had the nerve to giggle.

Claire shook her head, yet for the first time that day, she found a reason to smile. "Mom, I'm surprised at you. What would Dad say to a comment like that?"

"That your mother has good taste in men because she picked him. Plus, your father knows where my loyalty lies. What about your friend, Debbie?"

"Debbie Downer?" Claire gagged. "Ew…she's dead to me. Forget her."

"What happened?"

"It doesn't matter. It's one of those mean girl issues and it's in the past."

"What about Sarah?"

"Everyone is going except Portia."

The bell rang at the front door. Claire and her mother glanced at each other, wondering who was entering the bakery. The hour couldn't be more than 9:00 a.m.

When Peter came around the corner, Claire froze. He looked awful. Gray shadows lined the hollows beneath his eyes, fatigue wrinkled his expression. His posture drooped as if he hadn't been to bed. Had he slept last night? He hadn't chosen his usual business clothes, which meant he'd been at home. Instead, he wore a white t-shirt and a pair of blue jeans. A man who usually had a clean-shaven face had grizzly cheeks.

Claire liked the grizzly cheeks.

"I hoped to get here before you, Mom. Could you take a break? Go for a walk? Claire and I need to have a conversation. Alone."

"Whatever you need to say can be said in front of Mom."

"It's okay," Mary said, raising her hands, her smile fading. "I'll go to the front. You two need privacy."

When Mary left the workroom, Peter placed his hands inside his denim pockets. He seemed jittery, uncomfortable. "Look, I was leaving town, but it wouldn't be right to leave without telling you…"

He paused, not looking at her. The silence stretched while

Claire waited for him to speak, feeling like her entire foundation was shaking. She understood that serious stare. When Peter couldn't look her in the eye, when his expression furrowed with weariness and frustration, hearing his words could only lead to more heartache.

"I'm leaving."

Claire swallowed. She braced herself against the countertop, hoping this wasn't the separation she'd been fearing. "When will you be back?"

He shook his head. "Look, this isn't a business trip. We need some time apart."

"What are you saying? Are you leaving me, Peter?"

The silence stretched for several seconds, giving rise to an awkward and uncomfortable space. How should she respond to such a statement? Claire didn't want him to leave. At the end of the day, she wanted him to come home with her, but how could she convince him to stay? A wife should make a plea for her heart's desire, a second chance to love again, but the sad look in his eyes and fear of rejection held her back.

Peter stared at the floor instead of her. "Honestly, I don't know what I want, but *this* isn't working for me. I need more."

Claire glanced at him. Avoidance, her usual tactic, seemed best. At least until they were comfortable sharing a frank conversation. She grasped Peter's favorite pie, key lime, and moved to walk past him.

"I need to take the pie to the front," she said, trying to breeze past. "We'll have customers soon."

"No," he said, grasping her arm. "You have to stop, stop avoiding the problem."

12

The pie slipped from her hand and landed with a splat on the floor. Aghast, Claire brooded over the cream filling, white meringue, and a broken piecrust. Peter's favorite pie, splattered on the floor, symbolizing their relationship trouble.

Two hearts were broken. Lost. How could they find hope to heal the divide and rebuild their relationship? Claire collapsed to her knees, powerless to pick up the pieces.

"Let me help," Peter said, kneeling beside her on the floor.

"No, it's okay. I can clean this up. You're leaving," she said, whispering. Her voice came out strangled; her hands shook. He stretched forward, maybe to touch her, but then eased away. Claire appealed to him. "You don't have to pretend anymore."

"Claire…" His tone low, empathetic.

Her mother peered around the corner. Her concern mirroring Claire's fragile thoughts and emotions.

"You won't let me help you with a wasted pie?" Peter rose upward, throwing his hands in the air. "What do you want from me? I look at this workroom…I know this bakery bears some responsibility in our marriage troubles. If you were not here so much…"

Claire glanced upward, sensing his unhappiness, a look that mirrored her sorrow. Yet she perceived desperation and need in his eyes, too. "It's not only about me. Your accounting firm bears some of the blame." Her eyes filled with fluid. "What are we doing, Peter? Why are you leaving? Is there no way to fix this, fix us?"

He shook his head. "Look, I came here to tell you that we need time apart. To think. To get our heads in place." He paused. Was that emotion in his voice? Was he hurting as much as her? "My bags are packed. They're in the SUV. If you need anything…leave a message on the phone."

"That's cold and impersonal. The issues in our marriage are not *all* my fault."

"Did I say they were? Did I lay the blame on you? I need more. Don't you want more? You're not there for me in the morning."

"You're not there for me at night," Claire bit back, face heating. "It feels like you're blaming me. Where are you at the end of the day? Where are you going now? Is there someone else? A new bed, a new pillow to lay your head? Because you sure as hell have not been sharing mine."

He didn't respond to the taunt.

"She'll never love you as much as me."

"Who? What are you insinuating?"

Claire swallowed, picturing Lori. "Long blonde hair curled to her waist. High heels, fashionable blouses and red lipstick."

His face contorted in frustration. "I'm not dignifying that comment with a response."

"Will you be staying with her?" Claire took in a shaky breath, thinking the name might help her face the truth. "With Lori?"

"She's offered her couch."

Claire sniffed. Angry tears formed in her eyes at the realization of his probable destination. "I get it. You don't have the courage to tell me the truth. Just go to her then. Get out of here if you don't want me."

"Is that what you believe? That I don't want you?"

Peter studied Claire, seriously considering her while

waiting for a reply. The thorough scrutiny triggered discomfort and made her question if the implications for an affair were accurate. She had not witnessed a physical embrace, not even a kiss.

"I don't know what to believe." One of them needed to say: *I love you*, but Claire didn't have the courage. He might not believe her. "Does it matter? Your decision is made. You're leaving and I need to clean up this mess."

Peter backed away, increasing the distance between them. Her mom walked around the corner and approached them. "I've watched you fighting for weeks." Her mother's stature had never seemed so small, nor her voice so low and soft. "Peter, Claire, it's time to get help."

"Mom…" Peter gestured toward her with his hand… "this is between my wife and me."

Her mother grabbed a wooden spoon and spatula and came between them, moving toward the ruined pie. The frown on her face, and the tight hold on the implements, exposed her misery. The mess on the floor shifted her focus, but Claire knew her mother. She was determining how to fix the problem, their marriage woes, more so than a damaged pie.

Mary said to Peter, "When you married into the Davis family, did you think we wouldn't offer advice when times were tough? I know you don't want my help, but I can't stand by and…"

Peter placed his hand on his mother-in-law's shoulder. "I know you mean well, but you can't fix everything."

"Not by myself. If this bakery is part of the problem, Burt and I will find a solution. I'll talk to him. We can work together, so the two of you can have better balance in your marriage."

"It's not my work that's the problem," Claire said, shaking her head, "but it's just like you, Peter, to not admit that your work hours contribute to our marriage difficulties."

"Fair enough. I can't argue with that, but my income pays the bills. This work," he gestured toward the broken pie, "sinks money into a risky business."

"Whoa," Claire stated, wiping away a tear, "this is a family-owned bakery. A lifetime worth of work. Don't be disrespectful, especially in front of my mother."

Now anger crumpled her mom's face. Her cheeks blossomed with red. "Peter Douglas, I'll forgive you for that comment. Have you forgotten you had one of your first dates right here at the bakery?" She pointed at the broken pie on the floor. "Key lime has always been your favorite. It's a mess, but I can fix it."

"I'm sorry, Mom," Peter said, sighing. "You're right, but this doesn't change anything."

Mom went crazy. She knelt on the floor, reached for the pan, then carefully maneuvered meringue and pie filling back inside, leaving the pie crust on the floor. "Look, the filling is clean."

Claire didn't say a word as her mother spread key lime cream around the pan, making a new concoction. She spooned broken pieces of meringue around the top. "Of course, it's not the same, nothing looks or feels the same after twenty-some years of marriage. Look at my graying hair, the wrinkles beneath my eyes. I'm still the mother-in-law who was overjoyed to have a son like you come into my life, and a mom who has always given you advice, Claire, even when you didn't like what I had to say."

"Thanks, Mom," Claire replied. Sometimes, her mother's advice was spot-on, but this time, her advice couldn't make a difference.

Mary plunged the spoon into the mix and held the key lime concoction up to her son-in-law. Peter didn't know how to respond. His facial expression wrinkled in shock. Blank and unreadable. Mary said, "The pie looks different, but it tastes the same. It could be better than before. Peter, why don't you sample it?"

He appeared horror-struck. "I can't believe I'm considering this."

He accepted the spoon from his mother-in-law and tentatively tasted his favorite dessert, albeit, missing the pie crust. White meringue coated his lips. Claire would normally wipe, lick, or kiss the sweetness, but a messy situation didn't inspire closeness. Unwilling to take the first step to reconciliation, she felt frozen inside while staring at him.

"The standards have fallen a bit, but you're right. Delicious as always." He licked his lips and Claire watched his tongue, the longing to love him gnawing inside her gut. "Reminds me of an Eton Mess, but don't feed it to the customers. I'm sorry, it's time to leave."

"Claire…" her mother said, appearing as if she would hurt her if she didn't say something.

"Don't go," Claire whispered, hoping. "I need you."

They stared at each other then, neither of them speaking.

"Stop it!" Mary pleaded. "Don't do this. You love each other."

Peter touched Claire's arm, gazing intently into her eyes, and then he shook his head and backed away. "Time apart will do us good."

"You need time together," Mary said.

"I know you mean well, Mom, but I have to go." Peter paused at the entryway, turning back momentarily. "If you need anything, Claire, message me."

She nodded.

Peter left the workroom. Claire heard the bell chiming at the front entrance as Peter passed through the doorway. She grasped her head. Her mother stared at the pie, the frustration wrinkling her face. Mary threw it, pie plate and filling, into the garbage.

"It's over," Claire said, feeling numb inside. Empty. What would her life be like without Peter? Without his strength, his support, his love...

"It's not over," her mother replied, "but it will be if one of you doesn't try to work through the issues."

Claire looked at her mother, recognizing the concern.

"And by the way, this is a family-owned bakery. I'll talk to your father. He's bored at home. Maybe it's time one of us came out of retirement."

"That's not necessary."

"I think it is. Just because we're over the age of sixty-five doesn't mean we don't have a few more miles to go."

Overcome by the bakery's work and her marriage woes, Claire reclined in a nearby chair. The tears wouldn't stop falling. "Does Nora like pie?"

"She's more of a cupcake kind of gal."

"Hmm," Claire said, considering, wiping at her eyes. "Let's approach her. I have an idea."

"I do, too."

"What is it?"

Her mother came before her and grasped her shoulder, squeezing. "I won't burden you with the details. Not today. You've faced enough. Give me time to talk to your father."

"You're worrying me."

"My children are all that matter to me. I'll find a way to help."

Her mom assumed a contemplative look and then left Claire to take newly baked pies to the front of the bakery. Claire heard her mother humming and wondered what had inspired her sudden change in attitude.

CHAPTER THREE

*P*eter wanted to do something more than walk away from the problem. He'd given up too easily. Had the distance between them grown so wide that having a simple conversation wasn't enough anymore? The disturbing silence; the lack of laughter. One of them should initiate conversation. One of them should take a chance.

Why hadn't he?

He drove his Volvo XC40 along the highway, pushing the pedal to the metal, accelerating, driving in a careless way. He licked his tips. The tang of meringue pie still coating his tastebuds. His mother-in-law knew how to sweeten him up. He slammed his hand against the steering wheel. *Damn!* She knew her son-in-law didn't want to leave his wife.

What did he want? He didn't want to quit, so what had really coerced him to leave?

They'd been in trouble for months.

At first, Peter shared his marriage woes with Lori to receive genuine advice. He hadn't meant for her to get the wrong idea. Their conversations had led to shifting relationship boundaries, which could have crossed the lines of propriety, breaching Claire's trust. Lori's advice had done nothing more than confuse him. He had to get it together; get his head on straight if he were to rectify the situation.

Who could he turn to that would understand? That person should be his wife, or at the very least a counsellor.

Time apart will be good... Lori was wrong. They needed time together.

Peter had made the worst mistake of his life. The pain... the emotion on her face, he couldn't unsee her sorrow, her sniffles, her weeping. His heart constricted. His own eyes filled with unshed tears.

What are you doing, man?

Is it too late to go back?

He wondered, would time apart improve or complicate the situation, increasing the distance between them? His mother-in-law's point of view gave him clarity. There had been enough time apart. To work this out, time together—quality time—would benefit them more. What would Claire say if he went back? Would she accept him? Or...would she reject him the way he had rejected her?

Peter groaned. Emotional fatigue caused his head to ache. They hadn't made a physical connection in weeks. Claire hadn't so much as touched his arm or kissed him goodnight at the end of the day. Her kiss... They didn't sleep in the same bed. In fact, she was too tired to look him in the eye to know if he was upset. Avoiding conversation, he often came in late at night, and his beautiful wife, she was always asleep.

Sometimes, he'd stand at the foot of their bed, staring at

Claire. An angel asleep, breathing gently. *Open your eyes; notice the man standing beside your bed.*

Nothing was in alignment. Not the moon and stars, not relationship schedules or work schedules. It didn't seem right.

What was a man to do? What should he do? One thing was for damn sure, he couldn't accept Lori's offer, giving him a convenient place to stay.

He reached for his cell phone and punched the phone number into the keyboard, then waited for Lori to answer.

"Hi, Peter, are you on your way?"

He sighed.

"Peter, are you there?"

"There's been a change in plans."

"Oh? You decided not to leave?"

"Something like that."

"You know, you're welcome to stay with me. It's no trouble."

"Hey, I'm grateful for the offer." He lied to her. "But staying with you wouldn't be fair to Claire."

"What are you talking about, fair to Claire? The woman who won't have sex with you?"

Peter gripped the steering wheel. "Have some respect, she's my wife. You know what, I made a mistake. I've been sharing too much personal stuff with you."

He listened to the derision in her voice, the catlike drawl. "A man like you...your wife must be crazy not to submit. When you realize it's over, I'm here, my couch is here," she purred, pausing, "but if you need something more, something you've been missing, I'd be willing to share my bed."

Peter sighed. His guts twisted. "I have to go. I'll be out of the office for the next few days."

"A business trip or a hotel room?"

"Lori, it's none of your business."

Peter didn't give his office manager time to respond, he disconnected the call. The taste of key lime pie lingered in his mouth. His favorite pie. The confection connected him not only to Claire, but a family, too.

He knew what he needed; he needed his life back. He didn't know where to start.

Peter paused on the highway, shoulder checked for oncoming vehicles, then turned the SUV around and headed to Ocean Park. He couldn't go home. He'd told Claire he was leaving, but his mother-in-law had offered to help. Should he go there? He decided to stay, for the time being, with his in-laws if they would accept him.

WHEN MARY SAW her son-in-law standing on the other side of the door, his forlorn expression squeezed at her heartstrings. The fear, the anxiety in his eyes almost undid her, but she breathed a sigh of relief that he'd chosen to come home, rather than choose a place that would only cause further separation in his marriage. Mary took a deep breath, not wanting to submit to tears, reaching for patience and strength. Claire and Peter needed her.

She opened the door. "I'm glad to see you, Peter."

He waited on the front stoop, dangling his keys between his fingers. "I don't know why I'm here."

Mary stepped backward, inviting her son-in-law into her home. "I know why. Come inside, Peter. The kettle's on, and…" He didn't move. Just stood on the stoop, somber looking. What should she do?

Burt came up behind Mary. "Come on in, son. I know it's early in the day, but I'm thinking about having a beer, and from what Mary's told me, I think you could use one."

Peter stepped inside the breezeway, then paused in the entryway. "Is it okay that I'm here? I've let you down. I've disappointed my wife, your daughter You must hate me."

Burt grasped Peter's shoulder. "This is your home, son. Mom explained the trouble at the bakery. I also understand there might be another woman in your life." Burt said, his tone firm. "Is that true?"

Peter glanced away and Mary's stomach dropped. Not one to beat around the bush, Burt approached life's difficulties with a head-on approach. Peter opened his mouth but didn't say a word.

Burt nodded. "Claire's right, there is another woman."

"It's not what you think. I've been faithful to my vows."

"Physically," Burt said. "But playing mind games and picturing closeness with another woman, that's cheating. However, you've made a wise choice in visiting your mother- and father-in-law instead of the other woman, which means you know you've made a mistake."

"I know it's wrong, thinking about…" Peter glanced at the hardwood flooring. "I don't know how…or why, another woman *almost* came between us. It's made a bad situation worse."

"I'll tell you why. You didn't put enough effort into your

marriage, but we can fix this. When you chose to come home, you made the right choice."

Burt's voice had an edge. Mary knew he must take the lead, even if his counsel made her uncomfortable. "I need a coffee," she said, leaving the front entryway and moving toward the stove. She reached for a mug with a bright orange flower, grasped the coffee pot, then poured herself a cup of coffee. She normally added cream, but a miserable day had left her discouraged, so she left the coffee unspoiled.

"Take off your boots and come sit with us at the table. Let's talk about this."

Peter nodded, did as requested, and then walked forward like a puppy with its tail between its legs. Her son-in-law seemed to fold in on himself. The hopelessness in his eyes squeezed at Mary's heart. She watched him pull out a chair and sit at her plain wooden table, his head bowed. She felt helpless while watching Burt open the fridge door to retrieve two bottles of beer. He popped the cap from both bottles and placed one in front of Peter, then sat across the table from him. Burt massaged the brown glass between his fingertips and stared at Peter in a predatorial way.

"Before we talk further, tell us the truth. Answer my questions honestly." Burt paused, staring, stroking the bottle's neck. "Have you cheated on my daughter?"

Peter took a deep breath, then shook his head. "No. I have *not* cheated on Claire. I have been faithful."

Mary pulled out a chair and sat, essentially sitting between the two men. She couldn't bring herself to lift her mug and take a sip, but stared at the bleakness, the darkness inside the mug. A cup of coffee that didn't seem right without milk, much the same as Claire without Peter.

"Have you thought about cheating on Claire?" Burt asked.

Peter fingered his bottle of beer and then took a swig. "I admit it," he said, his voice a whisper. "I have."

"With who? That two-timing receptionist?"

"Look, Dad…"

"Answer the question, son."

"Yes, the office manager. I admit it. I could have gone to Lori's house today. She offered her couch."

"I bet she offered more than a couch. But you're here with us instead of her, so is it fair to say that you changed your mind."

He raised his head, looking at them, and Mary saw Peter's eyes were full of moisture. "It would have been the worst mistake of my life."

"Do you want to save your marriage?"

"Yes! Of course, I do. But it feels hopeless. Where do I start? We've gone months without talking, without being close. No intimacy. Little conversation. I feel like we lost something when Chris left the province."

"Parents can't place their entire existence on their children. The youngsters grow up too fast and they almost always leave home."

"I know it seems hopeless, but if you need help," Mary interjected. "If we could offer our support, to give your marriage a second chance, would you try?"

"I wouldn't be here if I wasn't willing to try," Peter said, anguish smothering his voice.

Burt nodded. "You can trust us."

Peter took a deep breath. "What do I do?"

"You start again, you build something new."

"You make it sound easy."

Burt reached for Mary's hand and she appreciated his hold, his strength, even his supportive smile. But had his advice influenced their son-in-law? Had any of this conversation helped?

"Did you think commitment came easy?" Burt asked. "Is conducting any type of business transaction easy? No one said that marriage came without struggle." He massaged Mary's fingers. "Sharing a life with a partner, *any partner*, requires work, patience, understanding and creativity."

"An open heart as well," Mary said, giving Peter a half-smile. "And hugs…"

"And sex." Burt laughed, winking at Mary.

Mary couldn't believe Burt had gone so far as to voice an intimate sentiment. She felt her face heating, her cheeks likely turning pink.

Peter took another slug of beer but didn't seem embarrassed by the comment.

"I'd like to contact a marriage specialist," Mary said, reaching for Peter's hand. "Will you accept counselling? Maybe an unconventional approach?"

Peter nodded. "I'm willing to have the conversation."

"That's great," Burt said, laughing, "because Mary has come up with a crazy plan."

"It's not crazy. It's a wonderful idea."

Mary knew what was needed to make a difference in Claire and Peter's life, and a close friend of hers could assist in achieving a creative strategy. The annual retreat's timing couldn't be more perfect. Claire's closest and most supportive friends were coming home to Ocean Park, and if the relationship strategy were to succeed, Mary needed their help.

She clapped her hands, fetched her cream from the fridge and poured it into the coffee. She took a sip. A delicious result and better than expected.

CHAPTER FOUR

*I*n the end, Claire decided her mother was right. Time away from her problems to attend an annual retreat would be good medicine, but one glimpse at her home, the place where she had built a life with Peter, carved a pathway of sorrow to her gut. Twelve days had passed since he had left, and she hadn't stopped thinking about him or feeling sorry for herself.

She missed Peter; his face, his blue eyes, his massive bear-like chest. She wanted him back. But what should she do? Call him? Tell him she needed a hug? A shoulder to cry on? Where did a woman with a broken heart find healing? How did she swallow her pride and reach out?

Without Peter, she couldn't sleep. This morning, alone on the bed, unknown sounds caused her imagination to picture all sorts of terrible scenarios. She wasn't all that brave. She'd better get accustomed to living alone.

Sitting in the SUV, she turned the key in the ignition and started the vehicle, then drove toward the highway, tears slipping from her eyes, feeling sorry for herself and not knowing what she could do to fix this. Her marriage was broken. *Reshape the pie*, her mother had said. *Create a new recipe.* How? It didn't seem possible.

Two hours south on the highway passed quickly, giving her much needed time to think. It wasn't long before she entered Summer Landing's laneway and pulling up to a cabin. She hadn't turned off the ignition when Anne came through the doorway.

"Claire," Anne howled, rushing toward her. "I've missed you."

Claire grinned, exiting her vehicle. "When did you get in? I thought I'd be the first to arrive."

Anne paused. That look on her face. "Well…"

"My mother told you." Claire shook her head, knowing she shouldn't be surprised.

Anne nodded, moving down the porch stairs. "Peter's the scum of the earth. Mother Hubbard didn't say as much, but I'm certain the tone in her voice indicated she felt the same."

"I apologize. I can't trust my mother with anything."

"Not where you're concerned, but don't get upset. Your mom isn't one to give up or give in when it comes to her daughter. The question is, what do you believe? What do you want?"

Claire shrugged, then leaned against the SUV. "I don't know at this point, but I'm not ready to talk about my marriage. I want to enjoy the retreat and not bring my friends down while dishing out dirt."

Anne leaned against the hood of the SUV. "You're not a dump truck. You don't dump your garbage on your friends."

"I hope not."

"Let's go inside. I have a surprise."

Claire grasped her suitcase and followed Anne toward the cabin. "I don't know. I've had plenty of surprises lately, and don't get me wrong, but I don't think I can take any more."

They passed through the doorway and into the cabin. A roar went up. Sarah and Laina dashed toward her and all four women were soon hugging. Claire closed her eyes, feeling tears coming on. Seeing her friends filled her with joy.

When the hug ended, Sarah looked at her strangely. "Why the emotion? Did you miss us?"

"It's nothing," Claire said, wiping at her tears. "I'm emotional these days."

Laina glanced at Sarah, sharing a meaningful look.

"What is this?" Claire asked, her joy at seeing her friends reshaping to sorrow. "Did Mom spill my secrets to all of you? Do you know my marriage is ending?" She dropped her suitcase on the floor. "Did my mother share my horrible life with you, too?"

They looked at each other guiltily, wearing pinched expressions, but not one of them spoke.

Claire shook her head and threw her hands up in the air. "I knew I shouldn't have come. I'm not in the right frame of mind to have fun, to talk about issues, never mind sharing the sad state of my marriage."

"It's okay, Claire," Sarah said, "you're not the first woman to have marriage woes and you won't be the last. We're your friends. You can tell us as much or as little as you want. Or nothing at all."

"I don't have the tools to mend a broken heart," Anne

said, reaching for a bottle of Baileys. "I'm more likely to grind my enemies into powder, but I am in possession of our golden elixir."

"Baileys is a starter fluid," Laina said, wearing a bright smile. She pulled a bottle of chocolate vodka from her bag. We need this bad girl. Girls, we need to have fun, let our hair down."

Sarah giggled. "As always, we come prepared, but a bottle of red merlot is better for what ails the heart."

"I can't afford to gain an ounce of weight," Laina said, her arms folded across her chest. "I've been asked to try out for the lead in a Christmas movie."

"That's terrific," Sarah said, "hopefully you don't have to show your…"

"My bosom?" Laina gasped, glancing at her ample chest. "There's no risk of that with the smash hit *Nativity Noel* being of a spiritual nature, and directed by the famous director, Joel Armstrong."

"I'm happy for you," Claire said, opening her arms. "I missed you. All of you. What shenanigans are we getting up to this year?"

Three friends cheered and clapped. "Just you wait."

CHAPTER FIVE

*C*laire watched the rising sun, its golden light glistening on the ocean. The waves gently rolled toward the shore. Yet the scenery didn't brighten her spirits; her life issues had clouded her mind. How could she improve her life? What part of her personal life, if any, should she reveal to her friends?

It was a mistake participating in this retreat. Her grief was overwhelming. Her heart wasn't into conversation. The impact of Peter leaving had left her frozen. She didn't want her marriage to end but had to face the hard truth that a future with the love of her life, with Peter, might be over. What could she do to make it better? Was there hope? Her thoughts kept rolling, round and round like the angry waves on a rough ocean, without resolving anything.

"So, this is where you've been hiding."

Claire glanced toward the sound. "Hi, Sarah."

"I saw you leave the cabin and I wanted to talk to you privately." Sarah sat on the log beside her.

"I woke up early. I've been having trouble sleeping, since…"

"You don't have to explain. You've suffered a terrible trauma, and given that I'm a nurse as well as your friend, I want you to know you can tell me anything. I'm here to support you."

"That's kind of you to say, but I need to face my messy life on my own."

"Sometimes it's difficult to admit we need help. Even more difficult to share our troubles with a close friend, or even a health professional."

"I'm fine."

"Are you?" Sarah asked. You don't seem fine."

"Sarah, please…"

"Look, I get it. I won't interfere, but I wouldn't be a friend if I didn't at least make the offer."

"You've offered, and while I'm grateful, I can't talk about this. It's too raw." Her voice rasped out of her.

Sarah patted her knee. "If you hold the pain inside yourself, you'll break your heart." Sarah looked at her in a knowing way. "If you change your mind, if you need someone to lean on, I'm here."

Claire's eyes filled with tears.

"Don't cry. I promise you; it'll be okay."

Claire nodded, wiping away her tears, unable to talk.

"Let's return to the cabin. You shouldn't be alone. I put the coffee on to brew. It won't be long until we attend our first meditation session."

"All right," Claire said, rising from the log, wiping away her tears. She stared at the pebbly beach and a manmade sculpture in the shape of a person. Inukshuks, flat stones piled on top of each other. The cairn represented safety, hope and friendship. But presently, hope seemed illusive. Yet thanks to her friends, Claire wasn't alone. She appreciated their support and hoped this sculpture put forward a positive sign.

A KNOCK STRUCK THE DOOR. Claire had changed into her workout clothes. She rose from the couch and opened the door. Caroline Dean, the camp director, greeted her.

"Good morning, Claire, ladies. Welcome to Summer Landing. Did you sleep well? Are you ready to have an amazing day?"

"We sure are," Anne said, nudging Claire in the ribs. "We need to get our friend onside."

"I understand. Your mother may have told me about your situation."

Claire shook her head, sighing. *Have you gossiped about me to everyone, Mom? That I'm doomed to spend the rest of my life as a cast-off woman?* "I hate this. I wish she'd kept silent."

Caroline touched her arm briefly. "I know you're hurting. I don't want to minimize what you're feeling, but there's no reason to feel embarrassed. I'm sure your friends understand. Am I right, ladies?"

Claire studied her friends' facial expressions. They glanced at each other as if they were hiding something.

"What is it?" she asked, frowning.

Anne grasped her left arm. "It's a fabulous day for adventure."

Sarah grasped her right. "But that doesn't mean you have to hide your feelings. You can share anything with us."

"You can reveal every bad omen that has ever hurt you, even your dirtiest darkest secrets," Laina said, facing her, "or nothing at all. We're here to listen and pay attention to your needs. That's what friends do."

Caroline cleared her throat. "Okay, I see what's happening here. Ladies, no matter how you feel, happy or sad, I want you *all* to enjoy the retreat. I'm excited to share that Summer Landing has new programming and new event venues this year. The camp overwent renovations over the winter. We built a gazebo on the east side of the lawn. It's tucked away in the trees and within view of the ocean. It's the perfect setting to practice yoga, meditate, or drum your cares away." Caroline grinned, imitating a drumming motion. "I've come to escort you there now."

Claire had no desire to ruin the retreat for her friends. She took a deep breath, hoping to bury her troubles. "Let's go. I'm looking forward to this."

"Really?" Laina asked. "Cause the tone in your voice leads me to believe that you'd rather go back to bed."

"I'm not that desperate."

Caroline said, "What Laina is trying to say, is that we want to bring peace to your soul, Claire. I'll spoil your heart and mind with wellness techniques, and your diet with proper nutrition. Not as good as the pies at Old Thyme Bakery, of course."

Claire frowned, and for the first time in ages the bakery wasn't a priority. A family-owned business didn't mean as much if it equaled a life without Peter.

"Sounds like we'll be having an egg white omelet with spinach and not enough cheese."

Anne giggled. "You're as skinny as a stick, Laina Anderson. You need to put some weight on."

"This body needs to maintain a perfect look, and that means there's no space for animal fat in my mouth."

Claire burst out laughing. "I wouldn't expect anything less from you. Laina, you're saving the animal world, one yolk at a time."

"That's right, sister. And I'll help you as well, if you'll trust me with your current struggles. Understand?"

"I do."

Claire did understand. These three ladies were her best friends. No conversation was off limits. But just because they could talk about anything, didn't mean she'd burden them with her problems.

The group left the cabin. They followed Caroline to the boardwalk, which encircled a portion of the bay. They walked until they reached the gazebo tucked away in the trees. Claire breathed the scent of pine, leaching from the wood.

"When did you build this?" Anne asked. "It's beautiful."

"We're proud of the changes we've made and can't wait for you to experience our self-care retreat. This is a sacred space, ladies. Come inside."

Claire climbed three stairs and entered a large circular room. Sofas, end tables, and assorted lounge chairs adorned the circumference. Five yoga mats were lying in the center of the space. Their instructor stood in the center space, waiting for them.

"Kirra will take it from here," Caroline said. "I'll see you after the session."

"DON'T BE SHY," Kirra said. "Come forward, select a mat and stand on its edge. Let's form a circle. We'll begin by participating in a smudging ceremony, followed by a healing experience."

"I've never participated in such an activity before," Claire said, feeling uncertain.

"Everyone needs healing from time to time. Let me bring the spirit to you."

Claire wasn't sure if she wanted to participate, but Anne took her hand, smiling in a reassuring way, and together they approached their mats.

In the center of the room, sweet sage had been placed in a basket. They each took a small bundle and lit it. Swirling smoke mesmerized Claire more so than the earthy fragrance that filled the room. Kirra led them in the smudging ceremony: "You can relax now…"

An easy thing to say. Claire felt anything but relaxed.

"Breathe deeply."

Claire breathed the pungent aroma of sage and perhaps the action, more so than the smell, encouraged a sense of calm.

"Circle your head with sage to clear your mind of negative thoughts. Close your eyes to pain and suffering, then open your eyes to a more positive view. Hear my voice, clear your hearing to ugly thoughts, to unkind thoughts, and hear anew with hope and love."

Claire swirled the sage around her head, her chest and arms, trying to release her anxiety. She went through the motions, motions that didn't gain peace.

"Breathe in," Kirra said, "breathe deeply of the serenity and healing aroma of sage and sea air."

Claire breathed deeply, her stress easing.

"You can relax now. Hear my voice. I'm with you. Breathe in through your nose, exhale through your mouth. Now stretch your arms above your head, extending your fingertips toward the sky. Reach, reach, reach…toward the ceiling."

"Claire, your friends have asked if they may surround you with their love," Kirra said. "Will you permit hands-on healing?"

What did Kirra intend? Claire didn't understand. She was uncomfortable, uncertain, but she nodded, agreeing to the unfamiliar wellness practice.

"Sit on your mat, make yourself comfortable and close your eyes."

While Kirra tried to impart calm, Claire couldn't relax. Though she knelt on the mat as Kirra had requested, wondering what would happen next. One look at her friends and the earnestness in their expressions told her she need not worry.

They looked at her with love in their eyes while kneeling beside her. Sarah placed one hand on her head and the other on her shoulder. *Had she done this before?* Sarah was a nurse, a healer.

Anne placed one hand on her back and the other on her opposite shoulder. "I hope I'm doing this right."

Laina placed both of her hands on Claire's upper back. Kirra knelt in front of Claire, facing her, then embraced her forehead and her chest, just above her heart. A profound sense of peace overcame Claire as warmth suffused her everywhere. And then, sweet music…a song she'd never heard before:

"How could anyone ever tell you, you are anything less than beautiful,

   How could anyone ever tell you, you are less than whole,

   How could anyone fail to notice that your loving is a miracle,

   How deeply you're connected to my soul.[1]*"*

"Breathe. Try to relax," she heard Kirra say. "Close your eyes, let peace surround you."

Claire participated in the treatment, trusting her friends as they embraced her with physical touch, hands-on healing. Not having participated in such a wellness activity before, she didn't understand the energy transfer. Heat radiated through her shoulders, enveloping her back and upper shoulders. Her forehead and her cheeks flushed with heat.

The music played on, singing a meditation prayer of beauty and wholeness. Was she beautiful? 'How could anyone ever tell you, you're anything less than beautiful.' Claire would never describe herself in such a way, no matter how many times Peter had complimented her.

Peter…

Tears escaped, leaked from her eyes and slid down her

cheeks, dropping onto her clothing. Claire didn't wipe the emotion away, but let the sadness weep from the depths of her soul.

Though she listened to her friends breathing, they didn't speak throughout the experience. They let her grieve and heal in her own way.

When the music ended and the reiki treatment came to an end, Anne, Sarah, and Laina stared at her with moisture in their eyes. Claire didn't know how to respond. What should she say? She appreciated their compassion, their freedom to touch her in places others had never reached. It showed they cared.

"Thank you…" didn't portray, not even by half, her gratitude for their support.

CHAPTER SIX

*N*ight had come. A fire blazed in the darkness, casting orange light on a circular impression of sand and stone. Claire watched the flames from a wooden camp chair, feeling more peaceful than she'd felt in days while clutching a mug of hot chocolate in her hands. Her friends had insisted she wrap herself in a blanket due to the cooler evening, and though it was summer, she welcomed the warmth.

They were quiet, and though the lack of conversation seemed out of place, Claire supposed each of them needed their solitude. Anne read a book while holding a flashlight. Sarah plugged into her smart device. Claire watched her friend tapping her fingers to a musical beat she could not hear. Laina stared at a black velvet sky adorned with sparkling stars, dreaming of who knew what. Their quiet dispositions gave Claire time to ponder the day's activities of meditation, brunch, and an afternoon dip in the hot tub.

Yet it wasn't catching up on each other's life experiences that she thought about now. The reiki treatment had warmed her heart and made her grateful for her friends. How did you thank anyone for healing touch?

"Claire, wake up."

She opened her eyes. "I wasn't sleeping."

"Your eyes were closed, and if you're not present in this conversation, you're not here with us."

Anne pointed at herself, giving Claire the impression that Sarah and Laina agreed with Anne's opinion. Claire sipped her hot chocolate. "You were reading, but never mind that, where's the Baileys? This drink needs a boost of flavor."

Anne reached for a bag. "It's time for marshmallows. They go well with hot chocolate. Would you like some mallow with your Baileys?"

"That's a flavor incentive I've yet to try. I've never had Baileys with anything other than coffee or hot chocolate."

"It's delicious. You have no idea what you've been missing. Come on, take a skewer."

Claire rose from her chair to place a marshmallow on a skewer. Three friends approached the fire pit and began roasting. When their confections were toasted brown, they pulled off the skin and filled it with Baileys. Claire put hers inside her mouth, tasting. She giggled when Baileys dribbled onto her chin. "This is the sweetest, most decadent flavor I have ever tasted."

"Would you like a second?" Anne asked.

"I can't have one," Laina replied, pouting. "You can have mine."

Claire reached for a second marshmallow and placed it on her stick. "Why can't you have it, you roasted it?"

"In a word, gelatin."

"Oh, that's right." Claire reached for a third marshmallow, feeling guilty for having one when Laina couldn't. "I'm having a third and I'm not drowning my sorrow alone." She watched the flames licking at the creamy white.

Laina rose from her chair. "Although it goes against my principles, for you, I'll try one. Only one."

"Really?" Anne said, giggling. "The animal rights activist will eat from the frothy trough of distilled animal fat?"

Laina placed her hands on her hips, her expression souring. "If you put it like that…"

"I'm sorry for egging you on. Actually, these marshmallows are gelatin free, so you don't have to worry."

"Anne, you tease, are you fooling with me?"

Sarah grinned, then placed a marshmallow on a skewer and handed it to Laina. "Your dedication might be growing on us. This Baileys is vegan, too. It's made with almond milk."

"Oh. My. God," Laina said, sampling her own slice of heaven. "I don't know what I love more, this marshmallow drenched with Baileys, or my friends."

Laina amused Claire. She was about to speak, but then saw Caroline approaching them. Their laughter stopped.

"Good evening, ladies. Have you had a good day?"

They all nodded.

"That's great. I have a special treat planned for you this evening."

"Oh?" Claire said, wondering what the surprise might be.

"We've had too many treats already," she said, noticing that the marshmallow bag was half-full.

"It's not food."

"What is it?"

"A night excursion to Daydream Island."

"After all these years, it's about time we went to that island," Anne said. "Is this part of the new development?"

The conversation stopped and no one said a word. Claire heard a pop and a spark drifted off into the night. She wouldn't admit it to her friends, but back in the day, Peter and her had taken a kayak to the island. The memory caused sadness.

Caroline cleared her throat. "Daydream Island is not part of our usual guest experience, but we wanted to expand. I thought you'd be the perfect group to give the island a try."

"I don't know," Claire said, studying the dark ocean. "I don't feel like getting into a boat at this late hour."

Anne poked her shoulder. The friend who had touched her with tenderness earlier. "You're not fun anymore. What's happened to you, Claire, are you scared?"

"Certainly not."

"Do you know how to swim?" Sarah asked, "just in case."

"Yes, of course I know how to swim."

Laina made a face. "We could skinny dip. Can you imagine it? Middle-aged women thrashing about in the water?"

Claire shook her head, laughing. "I don't think so. It wouldn't support your acting career if you were caught in a compromising situation."

"Swimming would be safer near the shores of Daydream Island," Laina replied.

"It sounds dreamy," Sarah said, sighing. "Not the swimming naked part, but four friends cuddled in their sleeping bags, staring at the night sky, dreaming…"

Claire didn't know why they were discussing this idea so late in the evening. "It sounds cold to me."

Caroline interrupted them. "You'll be sleeping inside a cabin with glass skylights. If you liked the gazebo, you'll love the cabin."

"It sounds amazing. Come on, Claire…" Anne said hopefully. "How often do you get a chance to look at the night sky from the safety of your bed?"

Claire stared at her friends' expectant looks. "This means a lot to you. Doesn't it?"

"More than you know," Sarah replied.

"All right, let's do it, let's go to Daydream Island."

"Yay, Kumbaya…" Anne, Sarah and Laina howled, clapping their hands. They jumped up from their chairs and danced around the fire.

Caroline said, "Your friends have taken the liberty of packing an overnight bag for you."

"What? You agreed to this without discussing it with me?"

Anne shrugged. "We might have had an idea you'd agree. You like adventure, after all, or you used to."

"That doesn't excuse you for not telling me."

Anne touched her shoulder again. "We know, you love adventure but hate surprises."

"Ladies, if you'll follow me, Graham is waiting. He'll take you to Daydream Island."

"Ah...." Claire cried out, "Okay, let's go. Let's sleep beneath the stars. Who am I to prevent an evening journey? Who knows what we'll find on Daydream Island?"

CLAIRE DIDN'T ANNOUNCE her fears, but she hoped she wouldn't face further memories from her past.

CHAPTER SEVEN

*P*eter stood at the dock, his bag held in his hand, remembering Mary's words: "We know this is an unusual request, but time away could be beneficial. Will you agree to an unconventional approach?"

Peter had stared at his in-laws, witnessing their hopeful expressions. He hadn't wanted to say no any more than he wanted his marriage to end. But the thought of spending five days on Daydream Island with Claire could either cause a fight, earning him a world of hurt, or yes, possibly open the door for compromise.

There was a benefit to spending quality time with Claire on the island. Neither a bakery nor an accounting firm would interrupt their relationship.

Though he regretted interfering with Claire's mindfulness retreat. Would she be angry with him, or with her friends, when she found out about this plan? Either way, it was too late for recriminations. In the end, he agreed to the counseling.

The motorboat left the dock and Peter listened to its motor as it cut across the bay, taking him away from Summer Landing toward the only woman he had ever loved.

CHAPTER EIGHT

*W*hen Claire woke up the next morning, her friends were gone. Although there were few noticeable sounds in the cabin, she didn't concern herself with their absence while brewing coffee. Maybe they were sleeping. Possibly visiting on the outdoor patio. When the coffee was ready, she carried a mug to the patio, hoping to join them, but was surprised to find an unoccupied space and empty chairs.

She massaged her mug with her fingers. "Where is everyone?" she wondered aloud, seeing a second cabin perpendicular to her own.

Carrying her coffee, she went back inside the cabin to check the second bedroom. It was empty, too. The beds were made. No luggage had been left on the floor. She abandoned the cabin and walked along the boardwalk that led to the beach, but except for one noisy gull, the rocky shoreline seemed deserted. The sound of the ocean encouraged her to walk toward the sea, to roam close to the water's edge, picking up the odd rock and shell. The wind blew cold, brushing against her cheeks.

What's happening?

Claire returned to the cabin, realizing that not only were her friends missing, their belongings were gone as well. She sat at the table and retrieved her cell phone from her purse. She texted Anne:

"Where are you?"

No response.

She texted Sarah, and then Laina.

She watched the screen, waiting…hoping for a reply, but didn't receive a response.

Maybe the reception was bad; maybe there wasn't cell service on the island.

She rose upward with her mug in her hand and walked to the cabin door and peered outside. *Where were her friends?*

Her phone beeped. Claire glanced at the screen but didn't recognize the number.

Your presence is requested at center court at noon. All will be explained. Wear comfortable clothing and hiking shoes.

Confused, Claire placed her phone on the table. *Who sent this?* What did the cryptic message mean?

CHAPTER NINE

$\mathcal{C}$laire went to the bedroom to change into more appropriate clothes. A simple woman, a pair of jeans and a plain white t-shirt suited her while at retreat. She retrieved the carry bag from the floor and placed it on the bed. Opening it, she discovered an envelope with her name written on the paper, which lay on top of an unfamiliar coral t-shirt. She grasped the envelope, pulled a slip of paper from its sleeve, and began reading.

Claire,

We hope you'll understand and won't be disappointed in your friends. In consultation with the camp counsellor and your parents, we decided you need more than we can give. You mean a lot to us. Everything we've done, we've done for our friendship. Your happiness matters most. Don't be angry. Embrace this opportunity.

Love Anne, Sarah, and Laina.

Claire let the letter drift to the floor, confused. What did this mean?

Claire took the t-shirt from the bag and held it in her hands, partial to the coral color. The printed quote emblazoned across a large white daisy gave an inspiring message: *Let it be.*

Removing her pajama top, she dressed in a white bra and the new top, then slipped into a well-worn pair of blue jeans. It was time to determine this meeting's purpose.

WHEN CLAIRE ARRIVED at the meeting spot, Caroline Dean awaited her guest. The camp director stood near a patio table in a garden space adorned with attractive flowers: garden pots of mixed florals; purple fountain grass, pink dahlias and various cosmos and green shrubbery. The presentation normally would have inspired inner peace. Yet the mystery surrounding this get-together made her uncomfortable.

Claire tried to smile, breathing a mix of sea air and floral scents. Caroline gave her a reassuring half-smile. If the look meant to offer comfort, the serious intent behind it only made Claire more nervous, giving rise to nerves and a queasy stomach. No doubt, her mother had instigated this.

"Good afternoon, Claire, I'm sure you have questions."

"I don't understand. Where are my friends? Why have they left me to deal with who knows what? What's happening here?"

"You will understand in a moment, but in the meantime, please take a seat. Your husband will join you presently."

Claire stepped forward, her face wrinkling in surprise. "Peter?"

"Yes, Peter, your husband."

Confused, Claire sat on the chair near the table. Her mind reeled with anticipation. Peter, the man who had left her, would join her. Why? She studied the immediate area, searching for him. A door closed in the cabin opposite to her own. Peter soon walked toward her.

He approached the garden space with an easy gait, wearing a long-sleeved dress shirt that lay open at the neck. He hadn't cut his hair in days and the dark wispy strands dusted his shoulders. He couldn't seem to look her in the eye. "Peter?" He paused on the opposite side of the table.

"Take a seat," Caroline said. Peter pulled out a chair perpendicular to Claire's and sat. He was quiet. Quieter than she had seen him. She always worried when their conversation succumbed to silence. Moments when neither of them spoke. What should she do, if anything, to begin a discussion now?

Caroline cleared her throat. "Claire, Peter, I'm sure you have questions, such as where are my girlfriends, why is my husband here, and what will happen next? Let me try to explain."

Claire nodded, glancing at Peter briefly.

"The powers that be at Summer Landing wanted to create a place on Daydream Island that was more meaningful than a retreat or spa experience, so when your mother told me of your marriage difficulties…"

"My mother told you?"

"Well, as you know, there's few secrets between us, and when one of us is worried, about anything, the other has always tried to offer their support, but let's get back to the point," she said, waving over a server. "I've been wanting to develop a couple's retreat, but wanted programming that would impact a couple's life, something meaningful and inspirational that might dust off the cobwebs of responsibility and rejuvenate a marriage. It's not quite counselling."

"What is it then?" Claire glanced at Peter as a server placed a beverage in front of each of them. She fingered the glass, noticing that he studied her in a guilty, self-absorbed kind of way. Had he known about this meeting? He'd yet to comment about it.

"Our new program aims to take couples on a journey. One, that if you're agreeable, the two of you will take together. You'll be our first two guests to test it."

Claire sighed, slumping against her chair back. "Did you know about this, Peter? Did you agree to a couple's retreat?"

He took his time in responding. He leaned backward, too, his hand on the table, long slim fingers slid back and forth across the metal surface. "Your parents asked me to come."

"You were pressured into it?"

He looked at her, staring at her for a lengthy period. What was he thinking? She couldn't guess what Peter might be feeling. His body posture didn't suggest anything. "As you know, I make my own decisions. No one pressured me. I wanted to be here. I accepted the couple's experience, hoping it might help us."

He hoped it would help them?

Claire took a deep breath, broke eye contact and reached for a glass filled with crushed ice, liquid, and mint leaves. She sipped, tasting mint, peaches and sparkling water, reminding her of a beverage she once made at the bakery. She glanced at Peter, holding the drink in her hands, feeling cold moisture against her fingertips while having a memory of one of their first dates, many years ago.

The recollection caused pain because she associated it with loss. But having Peter near, she recognized her love for this man. Regardless of what had taken place between them, she always would.

"We're about to take a walk down memory lane," Caroline said, clapping her hands. "Claire, your friends have worked tirelessly to build this experience for you and your husband. Hopefully, to help each of you recognize the weaknesses in your marriage, the mistakes you *may* have made, the successes you have achieved—together, and perhaps, how you might restore your bond. All of this to help you heal past wounds, which you might still carry, and hopefully recognizing the issues will help build a new future together."

It sounded like a lot of work. Not a retreat like she had expected, but at this late date, Claire didn't feel hopeful. "Peter must have known about this. Why didn't anyone tell me?"

"Would you have agreed to take time off from the bakery if your mom had told you?" Peter asked.

Claire thought about his comment. It sounded like an accusation. Peter often made her feel guilty for working extra hours, even though he had an excess of hours, too. "That's not fair, Peter. I'm not the only one who has made commitments to 'activities' other than our marriage."

Caroline gave each of them a look. "Listen, I will direct

the conversation, to keep the dialogue constructive, positive, and focused." Caroline stared at them as if she was their mother and the two adults sitting at the table were no more than children. "It's time to begin. Finish your drinks, and then we'll take a walk in our beautiful garden."

THEY WALKED AWKWARDLY beside each other, their feet crunching along the gravel pathway. The garden was beautiful. Large maples, arbutus trees and green shrubbery lined the walkway, giving them ample relief from the noonday sun. Yet sculptured flower beds and freshly manicured topiary mattered little to Claire. She only had eyes for the man who walked slightly ahead of her. She remembered the boyfriend who had held her hand on similar hikes. He'd pat her shoulder in a kind gesture, tease her, joke with her, and sometimes give her a gentle nudge that made her feel loved.

Where had that man gone?

She missed his touch, his teasing, even the embrace of a palm against her arm. She wished he'd break down the barriers and hold her hand. She frowned and glanced at the pebbled pathway, worrying still that he might be stroking someone else's arm instead.

Caroline Dean ushered them forward. She paused and faced them. "None of this would have been possible without your friends. You have good friends, Claire. They have gathered special mementos from your past to remind you of your life together, to help you walk down memory lane. Are you ready?"

Claire glanced at Peter. He shrugged. "We're ready."

They approached a simple white table, adorned with an apron to represent a tablecloth. A replica model of her family's bakery; a silver spoon and a business card holder with Peter's business card inside.

"Grab the spoon, Claire. Tell me how you feel while holding it."

Claire grasped the spoon and stroked the cold metal between her thumb and forefinger. It had an insignificant length. She studied the cheap white flower on a blue enamel background. A silver crown at the top. "This is the first gift Peter gave me."

"I was traveling."

"I know. You had taken a business trip in Vancouver. You'd forgotten my birthday."

"It's the thought that counts. I found the souvenir spoon at an airport gift shop. Sure, it was cheesy and cheap, but it seemed perfect for a woman who wanted to work alongside her parents at the family-owned bakery."

"Though you didn't remember your girlfriend in the right way, I appreciated the gift."

"You hated the spoon. Admit it."

"How do you feel, Claire? Tell Peter the truth so he can understand."

Claire placed the spoon on the table as if grasping the metal burned her fingers. "This spoon gave me the first sign that you didn't put me first. An airport gift shop and a day late." She could have said more. She could have told Peter that a silver spoon and a birthday were less important to her in comparison to him, especially after sharing so many years together, but she kept quiet.

"Peter, how does Claire's sentiment make you feel?"

"The ungratefulness doesn't surprise me, but Claire's right. I could have been more thoughtful. I could have given her the diamond ring she really wanted. She deserved my commitment, but it's too late for regrets."

"What about the business card holder, Peter?"

He grasped it, fingered it. "It was a great gift. I'd finished university and was searching for my first job. I struggled finding my first placement. Claire's gift gave me a reason to keep looking."

"Claire put more thought into the relationship."

"I suppose you could say that," Peter said, his tone somber.

"Did you find a job?"

"Eventually."

"Let's walk farther. You might as well bring that spoon with you, Claire, it could be useful for what I have in mind."

Claire grasped the spoon and followed Caroline as they strolled along the pathway.

"What year were you married?"

Peter glanced at Claire as if she'd give Caroline the answer. He frowned, then replied. "The summer of '95."

"That was a good year. I remember your wedding day. The two of you made a striking couple. Our chefs baked you a reminder of your special day. It's waiting for you a little farther down the pathway."

Claire gasped, seeing a replica of their wedding cake,

complete with their bride and groom topper. A silver-framed photograph stood beside the cake. The bride in her princess wedding gown and the groom wearing a smart black suit. They had been younger then, happier. A jar of mixed sand, mixed blessings, pink and blue, rested beside the three-tiered cake.

"How?" Peter asked.

"Your mother gave us a picture of the cake. Would you like to cut it? Maybe have a taste?"

Claire glanced at Peter, unsure of what to do.

"You're a pastry chef, Claire. You know how to use a knife, but Peter will help you; won't you assist your wife, Peter?"

"I can't believe it," Peter said, approaching the table. "This little scene brings back some interesting memories." He reached for the knife and grasped it, not holding it the way Claire had shown him too many times. "Will you help me, Claire?"

"Yes."

Claire leaned in close to Peter, feeling his right arm brushing against her left, while resting her hand over top of his, hesitant to touch his warm skin, though she used to touch him in a much more intimate way.

"Cut the cake, you two. What are you waiting for?"

Claire glanced at Peter, seeing the man she had married. "We can do this," he said, reassuring her. "It's just a cake." And together they applied pressure to the knife and cut through the buttercream icing and layers of cake and filling.

"Now, serve each other, the way you did on your wedding day."

Claire left the warmth of his hand, missing the contact, then placed a piece of cake on a plate and passed it to Peter.

"No," Caroline said, shaking her head. "Claire, you need to offer the cake to Peter, your groom, like you did on your wedding day. If I recall, you licked the icing from your fingers."

Claire placed the plate on the table. "No. I can't do this."

"Why not?"

"He's not the same man. He left me." She thought of the woman he might have left her for.

"This man standing beside you is your husband."

Claire shook her head, pivoted, and walked in the direction they had come, thinking she'd had enough of memory lane and wanted to return to her cabin.

"You can't leave, Claire. Not until you've served the cake."

"It's okay. Let her go."

Claire pivoted to face Peter, not liking the sound in his voice. "So that's the way it is, you'll let me leave?"

"Don't leave." Peter picked up the cake with his bare fingers and approached her. "I've given you a lot of understanding over the years, and I admit, some sorrow, too. I know I don't deal well with frustration. I know…I'm part of the problem."

"You didn't want me on *my* wedding day."

"That's a crass statement. It was *our* wedding day."

Claire pivoted again. "Admit it. I carried a heavy burden, and you didn't want to make a commitment to me, to…"

"I had good reasons. You were pregnant."

Claire splayed her arms wide. "I didn't get in the family way by myself."

"This is good," Caroline said, approaching them. "You're sharing the pieces of hurt that have piled on top of each other over the years. The sorrow you should have talked about long before now. You must confront the hurt to heal. Peter, offer Claire a piece of cake."

Tears glistened in Claire's eyes as he inched closer, but when he held that white commitment laced with buttercream frosting near her mouth, she did take a bite. He did, too. "I was a fool to keep you waiting." He dipped his finger in the icing and licked it clean. "When I finally had the courage to accept my responsibility, I met the most beautiful woman at the altar."

"Am I still beautiful?"

The question filled her with anxiety, worrying how he might respond. He took a bite of the cake. "A few wrinkles here and there, a couple extra pounds. Some days I miss the brown hair with all the blonde you've added, but if it makes you happy, it makes me happy. You look fabulous either way and have aged gracefully."

"Let's continue our walk on the garden pathway. Couples go through seasons of love and seasons of sorrow. I know you've had highs and lows in your marriage."

Claire gasped, seeing a tiny white diaper shirt and a brown teddy bear resting on a wooden chair. "My baby," she cried out, reclining to her knees. She picked up the tiny diaper shirt and held it in her hand. "You married me to protect me, my name and our unborn child, and then I…I lost it."

Peter knelt beside her. He glanced at her, then fingered the fabric, his thumb massaging her skin tenderly. "I thought you'd thrown this out. It looks like, like it's never been used. Why did you keep it?"

"I don't know. At the time I felt guilty. Helpless, hopeless. I had finally accepted that a small rocket man would come into our lives."

"It could have been a girl, a tiny dancer," Peter said, clutching her hand. "You blamed yourself, but it wasn't your fault."

Claire began to cry; tears escaped her eyes. She stood, still holding the tiny shirt. Peter led her into his arms. He grasped her chin and raised her face to peer into her eyes.

"Don't cry. Don't be sad. It was my baby, too." he said, holding her hand. Come on, let's continue our walk along memory lane."

She nodded, squeezing his fingers, and as if Caroline knew that this moment needed no additional commenting, she said nothing, but gestured for them to continue their journey.

Claire giggled, wiping at her eyes, when she saw two mugs from their honeymoon.

"Nothing special," Peter said, smiling, "but I had to have them to remember that day."

Claire smiled, sniffing. "I felt terrible tucking them inside my purse. I prayed that the hostess wouldn't notice."

A little farther along the path, Claire saw the gift Peter had given her when she'd completed her own pastry chef training, much to her mother and father's consternation, as they didn't think she needed anything more than family training.

"My rolling pin."

"I learned my lesson with the silver spoon. You must agree that this gift was more thoughtful and perfect for the occasion. Your mother loved it."

"This is good. You're connecting again."

"Your old briefcase. How did the girls find it? I thought you donated it to a secondhand store."

"Not on your life would I part with it. It meant a lot to me as I had just begun my company. The briefcase has emotional strings attached to it."

Claire became teary again. She paused on the pathway. "What happened between us?"

"Where do we go from here?" Peter asked.

"Farther along memory lane." Caroline gestured.

They walked past other mementos now, not saying a word. Seeing framed photographs of their two children, a girl and a boy.

"Stephanie and Chris," Claire said. "I can't believe they were ever so small."

"We're fortunate to have them."

"Conceiving was difficult."

"But with help, we had our daughter."

"And our son soon after."

"But our little family only grew."

Claire giggled, remembering their first puppy, a Yorkie mixed with miniature schnauzer. She paused on the garden pathway, still holding his hand. "What happened?"

"I don't know. Maybe we got lost along the way."

They strolled farther until they reached what seemed like the end of the pathway. Caroline led them across an embankment and lower still onto a rocky shoreline.

"Just one more object for you to see." A kayak rested on the shore. "You've taken this kayak out on the bay many times over the years. I've often seen you in it, paddling together. You can take it out now, if you want, cross the water to the opposite beach and end this journey. Or…you can agree to stay on Daydream Island for the next five days, continue to participate in the program, and see where the journey takes you. What do you say?"

Peter looked at Claire in a hopeful way. He squeezed her fingers. "I'm here. You're here. I'd like to stay."

Claire grasped his hand, hope blooming in her tired heart. "Me, too."

"I'll leave you two to spend some time together, but on the way back to your cabins, you might want to sample a bit more wedding cake. It would be a shame for something so delicious to go to waste." Caroline grinned as if the camp director had told a joke, then winked and left them where they were standing.

Peter picked up a rock and skipped it across the bay. Claire watched it bounce, fascinated by the ripples, while being grateful for this opportunity to tackle the hurdles between them.

CHAPTER TEN

*L*ying in his bed that evening, Peter recalled the first session. After Caroline left them, he had escorted Claire back to the wedding display. They'd sat on a park bench near the collage, eating a replica cake frosted with buttercream icing. He'd used his fingers instead of cutlery. Claire dueled with her silver spoon as if it were expensive silverware. The demonstration provided as much amusement as it did joy.

He'd watched her, listening to her, getting to know her again.

That Vancouver souvenir spoon held new fascination. He had regrets. He wished he could go back and change things. That was impossible.

When they left the wedding collage, Claire's fingers had been sticky with icing. The balm against his skin had scintillated his tastebuds, and the look in her eyes, let alone the urge to lick her fingertips, perhaps sneak a kiss, had been great.

But unsurprisingly, they'd returned to separate cabins.

Their reconnection had felt like a first date, complete with emotional outbursts and a lot of listening on his part, though unlike a first date, a married couple had whispered awkward goodbyes. Claire said goodbye and the cabin door closed, denying him entry, leaving him feeling alone. Worse than the loneliness, his lips were barren of a goodnight kiss.

The emptiness in his heart made him feel guilty for having left her in the first place. The shame weighed heavily that he had ever considered staying on someone else's couch. But they'd had a good start and he couldn't wait to see what tomorrow might bring.

CHAPTER ELEVEN

A new day sang with birdsong and the opportunity came to try again. When Claire approached Peter, he knew this couple opportunity gave them the chance to forge a new alliance. Even so, two jobs, his and hers, sat like a wedge between them, but perhaps their difficulties could be overcome.

Claire appeared cheerful and refreshed, her face enhanced with makeup. A slight smile tugged her lips upward, this pretty woman—reminded him of his first attraction to her, all those years ago. He closed his eyes, remembering the beach and a provocative young woman: long brown hair, eyes sparkling with mischief, and wearing a sexy yellow bikini. His gut ached recalling it. He opened his eyes, staring at Claire. The attraction remained, even with their issues.

"Good morning, Claire. You look beautiful this morning," Caroline said, giving Peter a wink. "Wouldn't you agree, Peter?"

"As beautiful as the day I met you." He wished he'd had the courage to lick the icing off her fingers the day before.

"Good morning, Peter, Caroline," Claire said, glancing downward. He saw the slight smile pursing her lips, and a welcome surprise, she blushed. Was she happy to see him, too?

"Take a seat on the sofa, Claire, across from Peter if you will, so the two of you can appreciate how good you look this morning. There's a fresh pot of coffee on the table, and our server will bring pastries, soon."

Peter reached for a familiar mug, not surprised to find it on the table. The two honeymoon mugs they had taken years ago. He poured coffee into each of their stolen memories. "Did you do this for me?"

"I wanted to look my best."

He had a sudden memory of Claire. In the bakery: flour dusting her fingers and amusement creasing her cheeks. He'd kissed her. He still wanted to kiss her.

When he finished pouring the coffee, Claire grasped her mug and studied it serenely, sometimes sending a provocative look his way.

Caroline cleared her throat. "You're radiant today, my dear. Our discussions went well yesterday, so I'm excited to get started."

Claire sipped her coffee. "What will we do?"

Caroline uncovered a white board. Holding a marker in her hand, she wrote on its surface: 'The Name Game'. "We're playing the Name Game. These are the instructions. It's a simple strategy. For each letter in your first name, you must select an adjective that best describes your spouse."

Peter glanced at Claire, preparing, wondering about the letter 'C'.

"Who wants to go first?"

"I will," Claire replied. "I don't want to put too much pressure on Peter. 'P' is for perfect.

"I'm not perfect."

"Yes, you are. You have infinite attention for detail."

"I'm a numbers guy. If I were to choose my own adjective, political might have been a better choice."

"If you're so well-versed in mathematical equations," Caroline interjected, "then you know you're not part of Claire's equation unless she invites you to do the math."

"I'm not sure I follow," Peter said, puzzled by the comment.

"Perfectly puzzling…puzzler could have worked equally well, Claire. What about you, Peter? Tell us about the letter 'C'."

"Cute."

"I'm not cute."

"Today, you are." Peter smiled knowingly, then added, "and tastes like cake."

"That's a noun, not an adjective."

"Hmm, let me think about this some more," Peter said, silently pondering. "Aha…costly."

"I beg your pardon."

"Hey, you said I was a numbers guy, and you're right, I am. But I must confess that it's not clothing or makeup that takes up space on our monthly bill."

Caroline wrote on the board, making a squeaky sound.

"That's a discussion for another game. Claire, let's move on to the letter 'E'."

"This one is difficult. Harder than I would have imagined." Claire tapped her finger against her lip, obviously contemplating. Peter watched her fingertips, absorbed more in the contact with her lips. "Elegant."

"I'm not elegant."

"You're slim, trim, you wear a suit like a dream…" Claire paused in her speech, her face went bright red.

"That's a kind observation. Does it embarrass you, Claire?" Caroline asked, writing 'elegant' on the white board.

"A bit. It does feel strange to compliment a man who doesn't want me anymore."

Peter grasped the mug as if he needed a solid structure to hold. "Have I said I don't want you?"

"Well, not in so many words, but leaving our home and our marital bed, a wife could assume her husband doesn't want her anymore."

The light in her eyes diminished, chased away like the sun slipping behind a cloud. Peter ached as if his own heart was hiding behind the clouds, too.

Caroline approached Claire, holding the marker between her fingers. "Say everything you were meaning to say, Claire. Don't hold anything back."

"This is embarrassing."

"It's okay. No one will judge you harshly. Peter will hear whatever you have to say with an open mind. Won't you, Peter?"

"Yes, it's okay. I don't want to hurt you. Claire, just tell me."

Claire peeked at him shyly, her heart in her hands. "You don't bring me flowers. You don't hold my hand. We hardly have sex anymore."

Caroline pivoted to her white board and wrote the letter 'L' on the surface.

Peter placed his mug on the table, reached across the space and touched her hand. "I want to hold your hand, hug you, too. 'L' is for love. Emotional and physical love. I want you. I love you; I ache for you. I'm sorry for not making a better space in your life."

"Peter…"

"Well said." Caroline nodded.

Claire sipped her coffee. "While I appreciate the sentiment and yearn for you as well, the word love is a noun, it's not an adjective."

"Perhaps our love will have to wait until we've overcome our issues. What about a born leader?"

"That's a noun, too."

Peter chuckled. "I wish I understood the language of love better. How about, 'lucky'?"

"Yes. You're one lucky man, to have found an honest girl like me."

"That's a fantastic adjective. We're lucky that your breakfast has arrived," Caroline said, as a basket of pastries and fruit was placed on the table. Peter selected a croissant and Claire reached for a raspberry and white chocolate scone. He couldn't tear his gaze away as she took a bite.

"Claire, it's your turn again. What adjective best describes the letter 'T'?

"Trouble," Claire said, grinning.

Peter enjoyed seeing happiness in her eyes again. "I'm not trouble."

"Terrible?"

"Hey, I picked positive adjectives for you."

"They were mostly nouns and I didn't leave you."

"That's not nice."

"Be kind to each other throughout these exercises," Caroline said, lecturing them with a pointed stare. "What about the letter 'A', Peter?"

"Annoying. She's always nagging at me."

Caroline stepped forward, tapping her marker on her thigh. "That's not caring for your wife."

"It was the first word that came into my mind. I could just as easily have said amazing or amusing, for the way you bake a pie, or the way you raised our two children, or even the way you used to make me laugh."

He wished he hadn't said it. The comment had slipped out of his mouth and it had clearly hurt Claire. "I'm sorry, Peter. I guess I must own my mistakes in this troubled marriage, too."

He grabbed her hand again. "I'm sorry. There's been enough sorrow."

"I need a minute," Caroline said, reaching for a coffee cup. She poured the dark liquid into the cup then returned the pot to the table. She added a spoonful of sugar as if needing sweet motivation to continue. "I didn't think this would be so difficult. It's an easy game. Select an adjective that describes your partner. I didn't expect the issues to pop up. I'm not sure why I'm getting emotional."

Claire sighed. "We apologize for being bad students, but

you're managing our name game fabulously. "C" fits you to a tee. If you were permitted to enter the selection process, I'd select your first initial as counsellor."

"That's a noun, love, but perhaps the camp director should have a greater status than an adjective anyway. Caroline, we'll be better guests."

"Okay. Let's try this again. Letter 'E'. Claire, you can't use the word 'elegant' a second time."

Claire munched on her scone, obviously giving this letter serious consideration. "I want to be clever about this. I want to choose a word that perfectly describes...Aha, I remember the way you used to embrace me."

"It's a verb. Caroline, can we break the rules on this one?"

"I'll let it go on one condition."

"What?" they asked at the same time.

"You must give each other a hug."

The comment left Claire speechless. She placed her scone on the side plate, seeming unsure of what to do next, so Peter took the initiative. He stood. He held out his right hand. Claire rose from her chair, vulnerability in her eyes.

"Come here, icing."

The comment broke the ice that had jammed between them. Her lips pursed upward, and she giggled. She edged around the table and stepped toward him. He took her into his arms, embracing her, placing his hands on the small of her back. Holding her felt good. His heart beat a little faster, a bit stronger, too.

"Now. I want you both to think about the letter 'R' as this initial is in both of your names."

"Should I release my wife?"

"No. I forbid it. It's been far too long since the two of you have shown each other any sort of affection. It's a crime. You're man and wife. You made vows to each other that you've forsaken. You stay that way, hugging each other, until I say you can sit again."

"The camp counsellor sounds like your mother," Peter said, sucking in an indrawn breath as his wife's fingers slid under his shirt. A daring move on her part.

"The letter 'R', kids."

Peter had a hard time following the instructions. He massaged his wife's back, his fingertips tracing the indentation along her spine to the top of her neck. Claire sighed when he twisted the strands of her hair between his fingers.

"Solid as a rock," Peter stated.

Claire didn't argue with the noun selection. Peter wondered if she felt the need pressed against her abdomen. Though the weight didn't impede their interaction. Claire leaned against his strength, saying, "Rugged."

"Doesn't describe me at all. I'm not an adventurous man."

"Give it another try, Claire. I can see you're both enjoying this moment."

"Rapture. I know it doesn't describe you. Doesn't describe me either, but it's a word that best describes this moment. I feel like I'm in heaven, simply from being held in your arms."

"Step apart now."

They stepped apart, reluctantly, leaving a slight gap between them. Peter saw the disappointment in Claire's eyes at being forced to give each other space. He missed her warmth, he wanted her back.

"How does the separation make you feel?"

"Lonely," Peter said, seeing a similar sentiment in his wife's eyes.

"Hug each other again."

They edged into the embrace and being held felt amazing.

"Claire makes a valid selection in her choice of the word rapture. It's a good word to use as a descriptor for this point in time as rapture has been missing. You have suffered a breach of trust, a breach of harmony; it's symbolic of your relationship issues. They began with a crack or a fracture in the walls. They widened when a husband and wife left each other's embrace, which permitted the space between you to grow. The mortar of your heart walls became fragile, permitting the dam to break. Your relationship suffered, gushing emotion, tears of sorrow if that gives you a better comparison. You can rebuild the walls. The two of you can rework the structure and repair your marriage."

"We understand," Peter said.

"Do you? Another lecture. You've let the space between you grow too wide. A couple needs to spend time together. Needs to hug. Needs to have physical intimacy. I bet it feels good to hold each other."

They nodded, and in doing so, both agreed that it did feel good to hold each other again.

"You've given us a lot of 'R's to think about," Peter said, hugging Claire. "You're better at this game than the couple you're teaching."

"Why don't you take your seats again."

Peter reluctantly gave up the warmth he'd been holding, realizing that Claire was crying. It broke his heart. He wiped a tear away with his thumb. He did what he should have done months ago and kissed her cheek. She mumbled a broken "thank you" and then they each took their seats.

Caroline sat on a chair near them. "How do you feel?"

"Like I've run a marathon," Peter replied, leaning toward Claire, "like I've been contemplating real work."

"You have. A good marriage requires 'effort', and that's my wisdom for you. I want each of you to give me one more word that starts with the letter 'E'."

"Though it won't always be easy," Claire said, "I don't want this experience to be our last."

Peter gulped. He couldn't have said it better, but they still needed to lessen the gap between them. "Let's embrace the energy we're feeling and make a new promise to each other."

"I'm all ears."

Peter slapped his knee, snickering. "They're elegant ears, too."

"Fantastic!" Caroline clapped her hands. "I'll take my leave now. Mark, our server, will assist you with other requests."

"What do you have planned for us after lunch?"

"You've earned a reprieve from your counsellor, but a word of advice. The couple should bridge the gap and spend quality time together. The weatherman forecast perfect conditions. Take a walk along the beach. Go for a swim. A couple's massage if that gives you pleasure."

Claire took a sip of her coffee and studied him in an intimate manner, a look Peter remembered well.

"No hanky panky."

"We're married, Caroline."

"You certainly are, but the gap is wide, and you shouldn't

rush to fill it. Who knows what random energy could cause more pain."

"I don't understand." Peter rubbed his chin.

"Then let me be frank. In my opinion, sex complicates things. I'd like you to refrain from intimacy until you've made a new commitment to each other. Can you manage that?"

Neither of them voiced a complaint, though Peter bore a dour expression and Claire seemed disappointed, too. They probably looked like disheartened children to the camp director.

"I asked a question."

"Yes, Caroline," they both replied, their smiles returning.

"Good. I'll leave you to enjoy the afternoon and leisurely pursuits. Thanks for playing 'The Name Game'. We'll meet here again, bright and early, tomorrow morning."

"What's on the schedule for tomorrow?" Claire asked.

"You'll have to wait and see."

CHAPTER TWELVE

They strolled along a rocky shoreline, walking side by side, carefully traversing the rocks while listening to the ocean. "I want to hold your hand," Peter said.

Claire looked him, observing his need as much as his outstretched fingers. She wanted to hold his hand, too. She pondered whether to say yes or no, but rejecting his request could create further difficulties, barriers that could strain their relationship. It was time to bridge a new connection. She slid her fingers along his arm, intentionally stroking his wrist. "I don't want more space between us."

Peter looked at her in a serene and hopeful way. When she touched his palm, Peter squeezed her fingers. "Neither do I."

She glanced at the ocean. "The water's calmer today."

"And the air," he said, inhaling, "is fresh and clean."

"I love it here. I've always thought there was no better place to retreat than Summer Landing."

Peter faced her. "Does it bother you that I ruined your

retreat with your girlfriends? You only do this sort of thing once a year."

Claire studied the waves, so peaceful and gentle, rolling to the shore. "It's okay. You knew about this, but the change surprised me. I don't how one would label the experience, perhaps an intervention?"

"It does seem like your friends and family, primarily your mother, thought something more than division was necessary."

"So, you did know about the plans."

Peter kicked at a rock, then looked out across the bay. "Not much, really. Only that you would be here, and we'd have time together. Time to reconnect."

"Does it mean what I think it means?"

"That I didn't want to give up on you, on us?"

"Well, you can tell me," Claire said.

"Caroline said we couldn't be intimate, but I feel a man needs to show his wife how he feels about her. Would you kiss me like you used to, when we were young and silly, and the world was our oyster?"

Peter's eyes sparkled with mischief. He smiled and for the life of her she didn't know why she hesitated.

"Come on, Claire."

She pivoted in his arms, wanting him, leaning her back against his chest, but desiring the truth more so than a kiss. "Peter, I need to ask you a question."

He didn't release her, but rather held her to him, his hands, palm on palm. She felt his touch against her belly. *Oh, my goodness.* The butterflies fluttered inside. *Someone give me strength to voice my convictions.*

"I'm waiting."

"This is a difficult subject to broach."

"There's no secrets between us. Whatever you're holding back, tell me."

"Did you sleep with Lori?"

Peter didn't speak for several seconds. Claire worried as the silence and the gap stretched. He released her, but then surprisingly, turned her to face him, his hands soon resting on her shoulders. She closed her eyes, fearing the answer to her question.

"Look at me, Claire."

Claire opened her eyes, witnessing his seriousness. "When you didn't come home one night, I drove to your office. It was late. Only your car and Lori's car were left in the parking lot."

Peter was quiet. He didn't say a word.

Claire took a shaky breath and continued. "I don't know why I didn't believe you. Maybe coming home late in the night...almost every night, caused doubt."

"You were always asleep."

"I pretended."

"You're the only woman I've *ever* had sex with."

"You were sitting at your desk; she was leaning over you, touching your arm?"

"I never touched her. You're the only woman I've ever held close."

His hand left her shoulder and found her cheek, her chin. She leaned into the warmth, her forehead furrowing with worry. She raised her sight to study him, to seriously scrutinize his intent. "Must I ask you again? Please...Tell me the truth."

"You were there that night. What did you see? A rollicking good time with twisted tongues and a hand up a skirt? I didn't sleep with her."

Claire felt confused. What could she say to such a harsh statement? "I didn't have the courage to watch, so I left. Tears were pouring from my eyes, making it difficult to drive. I'm surprised I didn't get in an accident."

Peter sighed. He released her. He walked to the water's edge and stared across the bay to the shoreline on the other side. Claire felt guilty for broaching the subject. There it was, again, that space between them. She followed him to the brink.

"Look, I didn't want to bring it up, but I need to restore our trust."

He forgot the rippling waves and came to stand beside her. "This will sound crass, but I only want to lie in bed with you. Claire, I've been faithful in terms of my body, but it's time for truth. Some honesty. I was lonely. My mind spun and my blood pulsed. Damn it." He turned away from her and in his moment of shame, Claire saw his guilt, but she let him finish. "I considered Lori; I contemplated her couch." He glanced at her. "My head was messed up. I knew it was wrong. I came close to making a bad choice."

"What stopped you?" Claire asked.

"You stopped me. When I could only think of my wife and how I would hurt you, or further harm our marriage, I approached your family for help."

"You did what?" Her voice came out in a whisper.

He grasped her arms. "Claire—I love you."

The raw emotion in his voice almost undid her, but she pressed on. "Why did that woman stroke your arm?"

"Maybe because I talked about you. A man seeking marital advice from the wrong person. It's clear to me that boundaries were crossed. I'll release Lori from her position. I don't want any more space coming between us."

Claire inched toward him. "Do you mean that?"

"Honey," he said, holding her hands, "what more can I say? I have work to do to earn back your trust. But I want you to know...I love you. I want you. I need you in my life."

"Then I say yes."

"To what?"

"To the kiss." Claire stood on her tiptoes. "Come on, get ready, pucker those lips..."

Peter smiled at her and the warmth in his expression filled her with hope. He wasn't prepared for the wife who launched herself at him. He floundered slightly on his feet but successfully lifted her into the air as their lips made contact. She gave him a long and affectionate kiss. She leaned against him, clutching his head, her feet dancing in the air until the kiss was over.

She lingered in his arms, clutching his shoulders, giggling. His laughter rumbled from his chest. Claire loved this moment.

When he placed her back on her feet, Peter clasped her hand in his own and escorted her along the beach. "Your eyes are sparkling again."

"They're seeing diamonds in the sky."

He squeezed her fingers. "I told you you're a costly woman."

"Do you want to see the fish at the dock?"

"I thought you'd never ask."

HIDDEN BEHIND A TREE, Caroline Dean watched Peter and Claire from a distance. They strolled beside the bay, holding each other's hands. The day had gone better than expected and she couldn't wait to give Mary a full report. Her friend would be happy to learn her daughter and son-in-law were mending fences, and as her friend, Caroline appreciated knowing her new program assisted in the process. The slogan, a sea for summer, achieved better results than either had expected.

That kiss. Wow… This day had been complicated, but perfectly so. She was pleased to see Peter and Claire expressing their affection for each other.

CHAPTER THIRTEEN

*C*laire was enjoying a peaceful sleep when someone knocked on the door. She rose upward in her bed, confused, when the knocking sounded again. She stumbled from her bed and grasped a nightgown hanging in the closet, then wandered to the front entryway while rubbing sleep from her eyes. She opened the door a crack and peered outside. "Hello?"

"Good morning, Mrs. Douglas. Breakfast will be served in your cabin today."

"Oh?" Claire opened the door, permitting the server to enter. He passed through the doorway carrying a serving tray. He placed it on the coffee table, complete with a covered plate, a pot of coffee and a single rose in a bud vase.

"I'm sorry. I wasn't expecting breakfast in my room, nor for it to arrive at such an early hour. I've only just awakened."

He grinned at her, his eyebrows rising. "I apologize for the inconvenience, but I thought you were a pastry chef. Don't chefs rise early?"

The comment irritated Claire. "I'm on retreat, sir."

"Not today." He laughed, and she wondered what the inflection in his voice meant. "Caroline insisted on an early start, and given the planned activity, you'll want to eat a hearty breakfast. You're to meet Creekside at 8:00 a.m."

Claire glanced at her phone, checking the time. "That's in an hour."

The server returned to the entrance. "I don't make the rules, but I am paid to follow them," he said, grasping the doorknob. "Caroline drafted a letter for you. It's on the tray."

"Of course, she has."

After the server left, Claire poured herself a cup of coffee. After taking a sip, she placed the mug on the coffee table and reached for the letter, then lifted the lid of the serving dish with her free hand. A full breakfast of eggs Benedict with a side helping of hash browns and an orange floret. She groaned. Not being one to eat at an early hour, she replaced the lid, opened the envelope, and pulled out a tiny sheet of paper.

Dear Claire, this is an exciting day! Please wear comfortable clothing and solid footwear and meet Creekside promptly at 8:00 a.m. See you soon!

"You have me intrigued, Caroline. What are you planning?"

Since the message implied they'd face a physical activity, Claire took the server's advice to heart and ate the entire breakfast, all the while wondering what would happen next.

Caroline and Peter were conversing near the creek when she arrived. Peter wore a navy blue hoody and jeans, and as Claire was accustomed to seeing him in business wear, the casual clothing caused her heart to flutter. He hadn't shaved and the dark whiskers threaded with silver only highlighted his masculinity and gave him a handsome appeal. She wanted to nestle against his grizzled face.

"Good morning." Caroline and Peter greeted her at the same time.

"Good morning, Peter, Caroline," Claire replied. Peter extended his hand to her, and she grasped it momentarily, squeezing his fingers. "I'm afraid to ask about today's activity."

"Ah," Caroline said, placing her hands on her hips. "We've had two successful days in couple therapy. Yesterday we identified that a space exists in your relationship. Today, we want to bridge the gap and encourage a husband and wife to work together, to lessen the divide."

"Sounds great, figuratively speaking, but how will you teach us?" Peter asked.

"I thought you'd never ask. Come with me. Let's walk toward the creek."

Claire heard the meditative sound of flowing water even before they reached the bank's edge, but a pile of timber lying on the grass drew her curiosity. At least ten logs were placed near the bank, which were approximately 8 feet long. Five shorter rods, which she estimated were about 3 feet each, lay nearby.

"What's this?" Peter asked, looking at Caroline.

"This is what we're tentatively entitling the Leonardo Bridge project. The two of you must build a bridge that will span the creek, and once complete, you must meet in the middle."

Claire studied the pile of lumber, wondering how building a bridge could be possible. She didn't indulge in heavy labor. Peter didn't either. Lifting pies didn't require much muscle and a guy who crunched numbers for a living might not be strong enough to lift this weight. The thought of the exertion required made her wary.

"What will this physical work accomplish?" Claire asked.

"I'm glad you asked. In the last two days, we identified that your marriage has suffered because a couple has placed too much space between them…through your work, by not sleeping in the same bed, or the same room for several weeks…"

"Who told you we were not sleeping in the same bed?"

Peter shook his head. "You told your mother."

Claire glanced at Peter, feeling deflated. "I admit it. I did seek Mom's advice, and probably gave her too much information."

"I don't want you to lose your focus, so let's return to today's activity. You are constructing a new hope to bring the two of you closer together. However, a couple cannot come together without work. So, you must put some effort into this project."

The construction of the bridge seemed like an impossible feat to Claire. Lengths of lumber were lying on the ground with no way to put them together. Perhaps she was being shortsighted, or too negative, but there were no tools; no hammers or nails, to bring the pieces together. "It seems impossible. Where do we start? How do we begin?"

"Nothing's impossible. One only needs guidance to see what cannot be seen. I have instructions for you. Who will be the project manager?"

Claire glanced at Peter hopefully. "I'll do it," he said, releasing her fingers. "I'm the numbers guy after all." He winked at Claire.

"Great." Caroline handed Peter a piece of paper. "Here's your instructions."

Peter studied the paper while giving her a quizzical look. "We have to place two logs, lengthwise across the creek." Peter looked at the creek and the flowing water in between the two banks. "It appears one of us will get wet."

Claire giggled, wondering about the water's depth. "I'm glad I married a gentleman. One who will save me from wet feet."

Caroline laughed, and her humor didn't amuse either of them. "That's not the way it works. Marriage seems exciting when a couple takes their vows, but marriage is messy, commitment is work, which is why Peter places one log and you place the other, both of you getting wet. I don't want accidents, so you'll attach the first two logs to front fastenings. You'll place each log in its proper holder."

"Looks simple enough." Peter tucked the paper inside his back pocket.

Claire stepped toward the creek, realizing that she'd have

to tackle running water to reach the other side. Even though the flow seemed minimal, she glanced at her running shoes, white socks, then the muddy shoreline on the opposite bank. She couldn't avoid her shoes filling with water, never mind the potential to soil her pant legs. "Damn it," she said, grumbling.

"If only your mother could see you now."

Peter placed his hands on his hips. "You're enjoying this too much, Caroline. How long have Mary and you been friends?"

"Long enough to know she'd be fascinated by this experiment."

"I suspect Burt would be laughing his head off." Peter looked at Claire then, a look of frustration changing to one of optimism. "Okay, we can do this. Come on, Claire. Let's build a bridge."

Peter picked up his log and she reluctantly grabbed hers. At four inches thick, they were heavier than they appeared. Claire struggled with the weight while trying to match Peter's pace. She dropped the log, but then picked it up again. Heaving, each of them dragging their logs toward the creek's edge. She bore the weight, struggling, pulling…and with one look of conviction, each of them stepped into the creek.

"It's cold," Claire called out, water sloshing against her shoes, but she overcame the chill as water invaded her sneakers and climbed her legs all the way to her knees. Peter dropped his log, causing the water to splash in her face. The frigid cold stunned her.

"I'm sorry," Peter said, then he picked up the log and they

trudged the short distance to the other side of the bank. They lifted their logs into place, wedging them in the support, and then stood on the watery break, their feet wet, their faces glistening with moisture, admiring the first step in their work.

"Step one done," Claire said, sighing. Though water dribbled down her face, she gave Peter a high five.

"I didn't know you were so strong. I'd have had you building bridges with me a long time ago."

"Where'd we put it? We don't have a creek in our backyard."

"You need to use your imagination," Caroline interjected, "but back to the activity, marriage requires a strong foundation. A bridge's foundation must be solid, too. Please give some thought to your supports, or your bridge, as compared to your relationship, could topple."

Peter checked the logs, then he winked at her. "Look good to me. Not so difficult. Hey, do you think we can complete the rest of the project?"

He smiled, although his feet were as wet as hers. Though Claire was cold, she smiled at him, too. "We can do anything if we work together."

"Let's get our first cross brace, shall we?" Peter reached for her hand, and she grasped his, enclosing her fingers in his strength. Together they waded back to other side of the creek.

Peter grabbed a 3-foot log. A slot had already been cut into each of the two 8-foot logs to receive the cross brace, so it wasn't difficult to place. Peter attached the first.

Then Claire grabbed a second log, and Peter did, too, each of them dragging their logs across the rocky slope and into the creek, and soon placing each log on top of the cross brace to the left and right of middle. Peter retrieved the instructions from his back pocket and stood in the middle of the creek, reading. "Now, one of us must lift the bottom two logs, while the other places the cross brace between the first logs. It might be heavy."

"I'm strong, Peter. I can do it."

"All right then. You lift the logs and I'll get the cross brace."

Claire grasped both logs, bending at the knee, and then heaved upward, then Peter wedged the cross brace into place between the slats. Claire saw the rise in the wood and how the bridge had begun to take shape. "What's next, Peter?"

He read the instructions. "We follow the same procedure again. How about I lift the lower logs this time while you get the next cross brace?"

"All right." Claire left the creek and walked up the embankment. She glanced at Peter, standing in the middle of the creek, his pants soaked to his knees. She giggled, grasping the cross brace.

"What?" Peter asked, his cheeks pink with his humor. "Have you never seen me wet before?"

She returned to the creek, looking him in the eye. "I've seen you wet," she replied, placing the cross brace into place and standing so close to him she could kiss his mouth. She remembered the first time they'd jumped from the dock.

"What are you thinking about?"

Claire lowered her eyes, still mindful of his lips. "Jumping from the dock."

"Those were the days, when we were young and carefree."

"No kids."

"No pie. No numbers."

They stood that way for a few moments, wet, staring at each other's eyes. Claire took a deep breath and spoke with her heart. "I'd do it all again except for one thing."

"What's that?" Peter asked.

Caroline interrupted. "This is not a time for regrets. This is a time for building, and you have four more logs to collect."

"So we do," Claire said, giving Peter a half-smile. They both left the creek and grasped their logs, completing the process until they had a full circular length spanning the creek. But they needed to lift the entire span into place.

"Are you ready?" Peter asked.

Claire nodded. It had taken a lot of effort and her muscles were screaming from the exertion, but the log closest to where Caroline stood, had been secured within the support.

"Well done, you two. How does it feel to have completed your very own Leonardo Bridge?"

Claire studied the rounded structure, seeing how the pieces of the bridge fit together. It gave her pride to know that Peter and she had shared this work together. "Now what, Caroline?"

"Now each of you needs to go to either end of the span. Peter, if you'll be a gentleman and slosh through that creek one final time."

"Of course." He gave her a ridiculous look as he traipsed through the water.

When Peter stood on one side of the bridge and Claire on the other, Caroline gave them instructions. "Now you begin to slowly approach each other."

Claire stepped onto the first log. The bridge seemed sturdy, yet she wobbled a bit. Peter did, too.

"Now move to the next log."

The incline wasn't much higher than the creek, but Claire glimpsed the water flowing beneath the cross brace. It made her slightly dizzy. She wobbled again.

"Now stay where you're standing and repeat these words to each other. Claire, you first."

"I, Claire, will make a space for Peter in my life."

Claire responded as Caroline requested, staring at her husband. "I will make a space in my life for you."

Peter responded, voicing the same sentiment. "I, Peter, will make a space in my life for you, too."

"Now each of you, place your right foot on the center span, then hold hands."

They did as instructed. Peter's hands were cold, but his expression gave off caring and affection.

"Tell each other how you feel."

"I'll go first," Peter said, squeezing her fingers. She was certain he was shaking. "I love you, Claire. I want to come home."

Claire wobbled on the log. "I love you, too, and I thought you'd…" She lost her footing and slipped to her left. Peter reached for her, trying to prevent a fall, but his effort only took him off balance. They both fell into the creek.

Claire gasped when she struck the water with Peter landing right beside her. They didn't hear Caroline's shocked cry, they only had eyes for each other. Both of them were soaked. Peter grasped her hands and urged her upward. They sat in the middle of the creek, cold and wet.

"Are you all right?" Peter asked. "Have you injured yourself?"

"I'm okay."

"Let me help you up."

Peter grasped Claire's hand and they rose together, not letting go of each other. She'd seen that look before, the one that let her know that this man cared deeply for her. He bridged the gap between them, and she moved toward him, too, knowing he would kiss her. He grasped her head, his hands wet, water running down his face. She wrapped her arms around him, hugging him to her, wet clothes and all, while entertaining a long kiss.

When they heard the sound of clapping, they broke free of their embrace. Refusing to leave Peter's arms, Claire turned around to see Caroline, her mother and father, and her best friends waving frantically at her. Where had they come from? She hadn't heard them approaching. And all of them were smiling.

Claire didn't think about how they appeared with their clothing soaked through. She grinned, grasped Peter's hand and stated: "We built a bridge and Peter's coming home."

"Well, not so quick," Caroline said. "There's two more days of couple's retreat to get through."

"Can't wait to see what's next," Peter said, holding Claire's hand. "I've been missing out. Claire and I should have participated in a retreat years ago."

"Maybe," Claire said, her heart full, "perhaps we'll need to change the rules."

Anne, Sarah and Laina came forward and helped them leave the creek. As they left the water, Claire saw that her parents were hugging, and it seemed to her that they were happy about the new foundation that had been built between a husband and wife, but maybe there had been something wrong with the bridge support after all since they'd fallen.

She'd forgive Peter for not checking it better. A couple still had work to do.

CHAPTER FOURTEEN

The final remnants of golden sunlight streamed through a current of sea air and breathing in its freshness filled Claire with calm as she strolled toward the place where the ocean met the shore, her attention on a circular ball of light and brilliant colors of tangerine and blue. The beauty of it all sparkling just above the horizon.

She walked beside him with the backside of her hand lingering against his fingers, all the while longing for more than simple touch, discreet touch, yet glad of his company as they came closer to the evening's activity.

"Will you look at that—your parents are still on the island. Your friends, too."

"That's surprising. I wonder if they're participating in tonight's session. The bridge-building exercise challenged our abilities well enough."

"Caroline has tested our thoughts, our physical strength. Maybe the camp director has an emotional contest in mind."

"My mother's friend has never been an emotional person,

often choosing to take a direct, albeit confrontational approach, but maybe you're right. Look who's joining us at the beach."

Sure enough, family and friends were gathered on the shoreline within a few feet of the ocean. Wooden deck chairs were placed in a circle and her mother and father were conversing with Caroline. Her girlfriends had already taken their seats. In total, eight friends and family were participating in their evening counselling session, and it seemed wine and beer would be in the mix.

Her closest friend held a glass of white in her hand. "Anne looks as if she'd stab a crab if one crept from beneath a rock," Peter said, smirking. "Does she still hate me?"

Claire wanted to say yes, but what would honesty gain them? She chose to take the easier approach. "Given her expression, you'll find out soon enough."

Peter grasped her hand and squeezed. "Frightful, by the look of things, but she's always had a protective streak where you're concerned. You're her closest friend."

"We're certain to face torture." Claire eyed Peter's expression, entwining her fingers within his.

"I can take it."

"I didn't expect my family, or my friends, would participate tonight. It makes me uncomfortable."

Peter's facial expression radiated curiosity more so than concern. His eyebrows rose in question. "Why? We've faced your friends' scrutiny before. We'll get through it."

"Will we? Anne doles out the truth whether one likes it or not."

"The facts as she sees them, even so, I'm surprised your parents stayed away this long, especially your mother."

"Mom likes to live in the center of my world. "

"She means well. But here we are, let's face the music. Maybe they'll surprise us."

They walked down three stairs, descending to the embankment, soon standing on a shoreline pebbled with stones.

Caroline broke away from the conversation with her parents. "Aha… here they are, our two most important guests." She stepped away from her parents while waving her hands and calling out instructions as if she were a music director. "Take your seats, everyone, and please…leave these two chairs open," she said, pointing at the left and right of the center of the circle, "for our lucky couple."

"Center stage has arrived, and here we go." Peter squeezed her fingers, whispering his amusement, then released his grip, glancing at her for a moment with a twinkle in his eyes. She missed his touch. "How difficult can it be?"

"Oh god," Claire said, looking at Anne again, "I feel like a puppet on display. I want to run for my life. Will you join me?"

"When it's over. Let's take our seats."

Claire sat, the deck chair hard against her buttocks. Anne sat on her left and her mom on her right. Peter sat directly across from her, and on his right sat Laina and on his left, her dear old dad. Sarah took up the middle of these two positions and enjoyed a favorable position nearest to the ocean. Caroline, having the best view of everyone, including the ocean, directed the evening's festivities.

"Welcome to the shores of Daydream Island. First and foremost, I want to thank my dearest friends, Mary and Burt, for giving me the opportunity to make a lifetime pursuit come true in our new retreat and relationship programming center."

Mary expressed a familiar sincerity, smiling sweetly, a look that warmed Claire's heart. "You're welcome, dear friend."

"I also want to express my gratitude to Claire and Peter. Not only for working on their relationship issues, but also for enabling Summer Landing to test a couple's healing experience for further guests. I know this guest experience came as a surprise to you, Claire, but I hope it gives you comfort that Peter agreed to my plans from the start."

Claire glanced at him, feeling emotional and grateful that he'd made the couple commitment. His effort expressed goodwill. He wasn't sitting beside her, but at least they were meeting inside the same circle.

"When in difficulty, a couple must have support from their family and friends, so I also extend my gratitude to Anne, Sarah and Laina, for participating and supporting Claire and Peter."

When Claire glanced at Anne, she smirked. Sarah lowered her line of vision, and Laina seemed as lost as a kitten or a puppy. Her friend glanced at the ocean, dreaming of who knew what. The curiosity must have overcome Peter, for he spoke.

"Caroline, you've held us in suspense long enough; the curiosity is killing me. What do you have planned?"

Caroline had yet to take a seat. She went behind her chair,

collected a reusable cloth bag, and pulled out an empty wine bottle. "Spin the bottle, anyone?"

Claire gave a nervous laugh. "Spin the bottle? My parents are here."

Burt's snort of laughter caused all eyes to focus on him. "Darling daughter, this might come as a surprise, but your mother and I have spun the bottle."

If Claire had been dismayed before, now she struggled with embarrassment. *What has my father announced?* She glanced at her mother, hoping to hear an intelligent response. Her mother's face, though struck by the light of a diminishing sun, had blossomed with intrigue. Could it be love? Mom smiled and offered a weak but musical giggle. "Burt, you're embarrassing me."

"I don't know why you're uncomfortable, Mary. We've come into the circle. Friends and family discuss such things. Be honest like Caroline said."

"Yes, Burt, and good of you for heeding my call for frankness." Caroline took her seat. "But this is my circle, my programming, and the conversation should focus on the couple." She smothered a laugh. "Parents do have marital relations." She shook her head, coughing a breath. "Which is why, in part, that Burt and Mary's marriage has lasted so long."

Claire shook her head. Mortified.

After she'd contained herself, Caroline gave them instructions. "However, we're here to address the issues in Peter and Claire's relationship." Caroline stretched forward and placed an aged, pale green bottle in the center of a small wooden platform. "Most of you understand the basics of this game. The bottle will spin, and when it points at you, you must do one of three things. Ask a question of the past, present a question of the future, or…tell an outright lie. Now, this is not the time for silliness or juvenile questions. We're adults; the lie must have a point. Teach a lesson in some way."

"A lie?" Claire said. "This is not the way we played spin the bottle."

"You were hoping for a kiss?" Caroline asked, her lips rising with her humor. "Regardless, your lie should be convincing. It must have a point for the couple."

"I don't know what to do," Laina said, rubbing her knee.

"You're an actress, make something up. Shall we begin?"

No one responded. Caroline approached the bottle, knelt beside it, and then gave it a good spin. Everyone seemed frightened, worried that they'd be the first to face the testing, but it didn't take long for the bottle to stop spinning. Its neck pointed at Anne. She smiled that type of smirk that caused Claire's stomach to tighten.

What would Anne say? She placed her wine glass on the round table. "I'm not sure I believe that a man can change his ways once he's broken a woman's heart."

"No lectures," Caroline said.

"Okay, I'll get right to the point. How can Claire trust this man when he won't sleep in the same bed and may have…"

"If you're suggesting I've been unfaithful," Peter said, his tone irritated, "you couldn't be more wrong."

"I meant to add that once a question has been asked, each person can only make one comment, but for this round, I'll give you two opportunities to have your say, Peter."

He nodded.

"How does Anne's statement make you feel, Claire?"

"Disappointed. I know Anne is only trying to protect me, but Peter and I have spoken about the situation with the other woman. He's assured me nothing happened. I believe him."

Laina broke the rules, grabbed the bottle, and pointed the neck in her direction, speaking into it as if it were a mic. "Do you love your wife, Peter?"

"I'll proclaim it to all of you. I love Claire more than ever."

The best news she'd ever heard. Her heart swelled with joy. She smiled.

Caroline took the bottle from Laina's hand and stood it in the middle of the circle. "Okay, that was nice. I'll spin the bottle again. I want the next person to tell a lie."

The bottle spun across the wooden table and it struck her mother's leg. She yelped. Claire was certain Caroline had forced the bottle in her mother's direction on purpose. Was everyone cheating? Mary picked up the bottle as if it was a living thing, and then looked at her daughter in earnest. "The baby never died. She was born in the early morning and you named your first child Lucy, after your grandmother."

"Mom—" Claire cried out. "Why would you bring this up?"

"If the child had lived, perhaps you wouldn't have drawn the conclusion that the pregnancy made Peter marry you. If it had lived…"

Sarah raised her hand. "Lucy would have carried on the

traditions of the family, of course, working in the bakery alongside her mother and grandmother."

"Please stop," Claire said, holding her face in her hands.

"We can't think of what might have been. I don't see a point to this lie." Burt reached for a beer and sucked on the lip as if stating a fact.

"I don't mind talking about our first child. The name put forward gave me joy." Peter glanced at her in a meaningful way. "We hoped to name the baby after my grandmother, after Elizabeth, or Lizzie as she was known. Doing so was important to me, as the child was mine, too, and I loved Claire even before she became pregnant."

"I never knew that." Mary sipped her drink, expressing her surprise.

"We never told anyone." Claire glanced downward, staring at the table and bits of rock that surrounded it. "There was no point in voicing stories related to the child after the miscarriage. But you're right, Mom, I've carried the guilt of pregnancy throughout our entire marriage."

"This is good. Not quite the way I planned for our discussion to go, but life has its twists and turns. Mary, will you take a turn at spinning the bottle?"

Mary rose from her chair and spun the bottle. There wasn't much muscle used in the spin, and it seemed like Claire's mother wanted the bottle's neck to point in the direction of her choosing, which turned out to be Peter. What happened next surprised everyone. Peter left his chair and got down on his knees. The agony on his face tore at her heartstrings. "Claire, it's true that I gave you a hard time when you told me you were pregnant. It's not you who should be carrying guilt, it's I. Can you forgive me?"

"For what?"

"For not loving you as a man should. For not jumping with joy when you first told me you were carrying our child. For not taking you to the altar sooner. For ever leaving our bed, thinking about someone else, and then committing the worst offense yet, leaving you. I should have worked harder to repair our marriage."

"While you're down there on your knees, this might be a good time to…"

Caroline pointed at the wisecracker. "I'll let you know when you can speak, Burt. Please continue, Peter."

"I'm sorry, Claire, for the hurts I have caused."

Claire slipped to her knees. "You're not alone in your pain. I made mistakes, too. But I never wanted material items like diamond rings or mansions, objects that only money can buy. Not even a family-owned bakery. Peter Douglas, you're *all* I've ever wanted. My only desire is for the man I met on a hot summer day at the beach."

He shifted the bottle out of the way and crawled closer. "I remember. You were the prettiest girl I'd ever seen. A nice smile, gorgeous legs, and…I couldn't get up the nerve to talk to you."

"I liked it when you called me by your pet name."

"Turtle? Really?"

Claire giggled, crawled across the wooden table and urged the bottle aside, and then reached toward him, soon clutching his fingers. "Despite your thoughts of someone else, I love you, Peter."

"Makes me sick to watch my friend crawling back to the man who broke her heart."

"Look," Burt said, staring at the circle of friends, "I didn't come here as much for Claire as I did for Peter. This many women at a tea party makes a man uncomfortable, and I didn't want the poor guy surrounded by a gaggle of vengeful women."

"Burt!" Mary complained.

He raised his hand. "Hear me out, Mary. Look, I know how you women let sinful pictures roil round and round in your heads. But Peter has been faithful to his marriage and I'm here to support him."

"My dad doesn't have outbursts for just anyone, Peter. You and me against the world? Do you think we can muddle through, somehow?"

"I'm here," Peter said, clutching her hand while nodding at Burt in gratitude. "I'm willing to try."

"Take your seats, kids. It's time to spin the bottle again."

But Sarah must have been over the 'spin the bottle' game, for she grabbed the bottle, rose from her chair, and placed it beyond their reach. "I'm a healer, and I don't believe spinning glass is the best way to assist or help my friends."

"Okay," Caroline said, sighing, expressing her irritation, "do you have something better in mind?"

Sarah pulled a rose heart from her pocket. "Yes, I do. Rose quartz restores trust and harmony in relationships."

"Hogwash," Burt stated, taking another sip of beer. "I like a commonsense approach, myself."

"Whatever you believe doesn't matter. This gift is used to

open the heart; to promote love, friendship, and feelings of peace."

Caroline sighed. "I liked my bottle concept, thinking you'd enjoy the spin, but how would we manage your quartz heart in this circle."

"We'd use the same concept, but each person would hold the heart in their hand, associating it with the couple, or joined heart, the idea of two becoming one, meant to protect and heal. That's what we're here to do, right? We're trying to help heal Peter and Claire's relationship wounds, instead of passing on our judgment."

"Okay, pass the heart to Claire."

Sarah did as asked and then sat.

Claire shifted away from Peter and sat near the round table. She massaged the stone in her hands. "It's nice to touch."

"What do you want from the future?" Caroline asked.

Claire stared at Peter, studying his face, his five o'clock shadow and hazel eyes that seemed warm and welcoming. "I want to grow old with this man."

"What does the circle say to that?"

"I'll speak up." Sarah went behind Claire's chair. She felt her friend's hands on her shoulders. "This is what I want for you. When you're old and gray, sitting in your rocking chair and rocking your grandbabies in your arms, I want to be there with you."

"Fudge and Jiminy Cricket." Anne stood. "Such a lovely picture you've painted, Sarah. I'll be the first to admit when I'm wrong." She placed her hands on her waist. "I'll bring the booze. I'm sorry, Peter. It's just that…"

"He knows," Caroline replied. "No more regrets. No more name calling. Henceforth, this family of friends goes forward, putting the past in the past and working toward the future."

It went this way until friends and family grew tired of passing the heart. They moved the round table onto the lawn and retreated to the fire pit. Soon, a large fire burned in its impression, sparks drifted into the night. Conversation about the past shifted to happier memories, inspiring laughter and long-forgotten stories.

Much healing had been done on this evening and Claire appreciated everyone who had come into the circle, bridging the past with the future. Exhaustion overwhelmed her. All this work made her wonder. What comes next?

CHAPTER FIFTEEN

*P*eter stood beside Claire, watching the motorboat take her friends and parents back to the main camp on the other side of the bay. The boat motored into the night, leaving a frothy path in its wake. Peter pulled her into his arms.

"Are you cold?"

"A little."

"Come. I'll escort you to your cabin."

Peter grasped her hand and she appreciated the simple contact as they left the dock and made their way, both of them quiet. Sensual need, shaped by love, stimulated a natural bridge between them. She didn't know how to broach the subject of intimacy, but as Peter glanced at her, an unmistakable look brightened his eyes. Was that need? Did he want her? When they reached her cabin door, he urged her to face him and held both of her hands.

"I feel like a portrait of my younger self, a nervous young

man, standing on the porch of your parents' home, hoping you'll invite me inside."

Claire licked her lips. "Why don't you ask me? See what I have to say."

"I was worried you'd say no, that you might not be ready to resume a more sensual relationship."

Claire released Peter's hand and cupped his cheek. "Nothing has changed. I still want you. I'll always want you. You're my husband. You're not a young, frightened boy anymore."

He grinned. Laughter resounded from his chest, giving off a musical sound. "I was never afraid."

"Nervousness then? I distinctly remember," Claire said, trying to muster up her sexiest voice, "sweaty palms and sloppy kisses."

"My kisses were never sloppy." His forehead pressed against her own and the contact warmed her heart.

"I miss your kisses."

He pressed closer, raising her chin, perhaps to see her eyes better. "What else do you miss?"

"My husband lying beside me, holding me in his arms."

"I could fix that, but are you ready?"

She nodded.

He studied her earnestly, as if afraid she'd change her mind, but this man who stood beside her meant everything, her beating heart, her reason for living. It was time to live as one instead of two. "Come inside with your wife, Peter. Stay the night. My arms have been empty far too long."

She grasped the door handle and opened the door. Peter followed her inside the cabin. He cupped her neck, his fingers slid into her hair. When he urged her toward his lips, she surrendered to temptation, kissing him, heating from his kisses.

The boy had grown into a man. His kisses were passionate, earnest in his need as if his heart and soul had been starved of affection. Need fired between them. Tender emotion given through physical touch, a stroke, a caress, tingled and hugged her skin, hastening her desire. She wanted him and welcomed the embrace; never wanting to leave the love they'd rekindled.

"I love you, Peter."

He swung her into his arms. "Oh, my darling, I love you, too." His breath whispered against her throat and she longed for so much more.

CHAPTER SIXTEEN

When Claire awoke the next morning, Peter had left the bed. An indentation in the sheets laid bare the place where he had been. She touched it, finding the hollow cold. Had he left without saying goodbye?

"Did you think I'd leave so soon?" Peter asked mischievously. He wore boxer shorts and carried a steaming cup of coffee in his hands.

"Well…" Where were these fears coming from?

"Be honest with me."

She patted the barren spot in the sheets. "Okay, I admit it, I thought you had left."

He passed her the mug of coffee and then sat on the edge of the bed. "I woke early," he said studying her face. "I watched you while you were sleeping."

Claire took a sip. "What did you see? Wrinkles, extra weight, a few gray hairs?"

He licked his lips. "I saw an angel. There's been changes. Your hair color is changing and you're carrying extra weight around the middle." He patted his stomach. "I have a few extra pounds in the middle in case you haven't noticed."

Claire took a second sip of coffee while studying the slack skin beneath his eyes, salt and pepper hair and the odd wrinkle, but his hazel eyes held the same expression of intrigue that had fascinated her when they were young and foolish, and deeply in love. From the deepest reaches of her soul, she'd love this man until she left this earth.

"You seem so serious. I have to know what you're thinking."

Claire rose upward and braced herself against the bed. "I love you, Peter Douglas, with all my heart."

He reached forward and drew a strand of hair away from her eyes, then tucked the length behind her ears. "I love you, too, Claire. So much."

And then he kissed her.

CHAPTER SEVENTEEN

When Claire and Peter reached their daily meeting spot in the garden, Caroline was waiting for them. The camp director held a cheerful disposition. She rose from her chair. "Good morning. How are my guests? Did you have a good night's sleep?"

Claire glanced at Peter, hoping nothing would happen to destroy the happiness they had built together. "Yes, we did."

Caroline pointed at the table and urged them to take a seat. Peter pulled out a chair for Claire and she sat. The server brought coffee, orange juice, and a fresh assortment of pastries. All three of them were soon enjoying breakfast.

"It's our last day together," Caroline said, sitting again. "I thought we'd have a casual morning, talking about strategies you can use after you leave Daydream Island."

Claire didn't want to leave. "I'm not sure I'm ready to leave the island." She glanced at the love of her life, her soulmate, grateful for their renewed bond. Losing him again would destroy her. As if Peter recognized her anxiety, he grasped her hand and squeezed her fingers. "Prior to this retreat, I thought our marriage was over, but now it feels like we have a real chance at happiness."

"I'm glad to hear it. Now for a few more pieces of advice."

Claire looked at Peter for support. "We've got this, don't worry."

"Peter, do you set financial goals for your company?"

"The business wouldn't be successful if I didn't have long-term planning."

"And what about you, Claire, do you make pie charts, sales strategies, or other plans for the bakery?"

"Yes, I do. Mom and I carefully manage the financials to ensure the business makes a profit and is sustainable in the long term."

"That's great. You should manage your relationship in a similar way. After the work we've done together, your marriage will feel brand new, and while you've given yourselves a great start, plans should be made to enjoy your future. This question might come as a surprise, but what relationship goals do you have for your marriage?"

"Well…" Claire stammered, pondering the question. She glanced at Peter, hoping he'd have a brilliant response to Caroline's question, but he shrugged, which disappointed her. After twenty-five years of marriage, why was it so difficult to state their couple goals?

Peter sighed. "After all the lessons, it seems neither of us knows what to say."

"That's okay. When you're too close to any subject,

sometimes emotion sits between a couple like a wedge. Let me help," Caroline said. "There are two people in your relationship. Each of you must put the other first. Do you think that's possible?"

Some habits were difficult to break. Instead of focusing on their relationship, Claire thought of the bakery and the continuous work required to grow the business. She glanced at Peter, wondering if he was crunching numbers in his mind, even though he sat beside her eating a scone. His expression became serious.

Peter grabbed her hand and squeezed her fingers. "I know it won't be easy. Nothing worth having *ever* comes easy. Effort is required to achieve meaningful change and I'm willing to do my part. Whatever it takes." Peter looked at her, his heart in his hands. "I love you, Claire. You come first in my life, and to make this happen, I'll spend less time at the office." Her heart beat a little easier and her worries lessened, after hearing his plea.

Caroline tapped her pen on a journal. "It's great to voice the plan, but if you're to sustain a realistic approach, how will you balance your workload with your personal life?"

"I've been considering my business responsibilities over the past few days. I'm contemplating taking on a partner to lessen the workload. I'll bring less income home, but I'll have more time with my wife."

The news surprised her. Claire hadn't expected that he would make such a change in his business affairs.

"What about you, Claire?"

"I need to think about this," she said, glancing at her

fingers. "The bakery has a smaller profit margin than Peter's accounting firm. But my mother and I have considered hiring Nora. She's shown interest in the bakery, though I'm not sure about some of her ideas."

"You'll have to accept some changes to make progress at the bakery, but you'll have the support from the original owners…your parents."

"Of course, it's their business."

"You're on the right track with goal number one," Caroline said. "Can you both agree that you'll find a way to lessen your workloads so you can spend more time together?"

"Yes," Claire and Peter said at the same time. He had a huge smile on his face and that look gave her hope, brightened her outlook on their life together, and made her feel as if anything was possible. Doable.

"Now that you'll have more time to strengthen the work that began here, what do you think you'll do with your time?"

It had been so long since they'd shared meaningful activities, Claire didn't know how to respond. Peter squeezed her fingers, giving her support through the action. "I'd like to go for walks on the beach. Maybe take the kayak out and sail to Daydream Island once in awhile."

"We could date again," Claire suggested, smiling. "Go for coffee; the occasional lunch."

"What about a romantic dinner for two?" Peter said enthusiastically, throwing her a kiss. "You know what they say, romance never goes out of style."

"Life is an adventure," Caroline said. "It's better as a shared experience. When was the last time the two of you took a vacation?"

Claire couldn't recall. "It's been years. We used to take the kids to places like Disneyland and Hawaii."

"We could again." Peter said.

"Do you think they'd want to experience a family vacation?" Claire asked. "Steph and Chris never expressed an interest to join us when they became adults. Besides that, we're stuffy old parents."

"Let's ask them the next time we talk."

Caroline closed her journal and placed it on the table. "You should start with the two of you before you invite the kids. Now, I don't want to cause embarrassment, but you should plan for intimate experiences as well."

Claire blushed, thinking about the previous night. "Are you talking about physical pleasure?"

"Intimate interactions are not always engaged through touch. True intimacy connects partners. It's marked by affection and love, which could include physical touching."

"How can you tell the difference?" Peter asked.

"Isn't it obvious? You can't stop staring at your wife, neither can your wife stop staring at you, or holding your hand. Frankly, the intimacy you're engaging in, right now, gives me joy. I hope it does the same for you."

No truer sentiment had ever been expressed. The courtyard and the ocean beyond might have been the perfect backdrop for this moment, but Claire only had eyes for Peter. He seemed relaxed. His cotton shirt, untucked, open at the neck. His hand on his leg. Handsome. After all the passing years, he still took her breath away.

"I'm bursting with happiness. It's as if I've rediscovered something rare and precious. These meetings have helped me to dust off the cobwebs of sorrow. It feels like our love is shiny and new."

"That's fantastic. If the retreat experience has made a difference, then I'm delighted. I want you to think of personal ways to show intimacy."

"What do you think we should do?" Peter asked.

"You could write love letters to each other, or lines of poetry."

Claire giggled, wondering how she would start. "I've never done that before, but it might be more interesting than writing a recipe card."

Caroline smiled. "You could massage Peter until your fingers cramp. Show him how much you love him, not just tell him."

Peter winked at her. "It's not all about me. I could rub your feet."

"Really? I don't see that happening."

"It's happening. Later…if you're willing."

Caroline chuckled, then took a sip of her coffee. "I want to end our discussion on a happy note. I want the two of you to always remind yourselves why you fell in love in the first place."

"This will sound scandalous, but Peter has a nice butt."

"And your legs…shapely, all the way to your feet."

"Let's face it, you're not looking at my feet."

"You're right." Peter leaned forward and touched her nose. "I was attracted to this pretty face with a few freckles, right on the bridge of your nose."

"Your parents will be pleased to see the work you have done to come together as a couple."

"Thank you, Caroline, for everything you have given us."

"You're welcome. Before I leave you, I want to share some advice about reminding yourself why you fell in love in the first place."

"You have our full attention," Peter said.

"You probably have years of pictures. Pull out the albums and look at the images. Remember and share the stories of your lives, your lived experiences together."

"The sad times, too?" Claire asked. She didn't want to remember the sad times. Never wanted to cry again.

"Especially the sad. Wisdom should come from happy and difficult memories. Just engage in all discussions with sensitivity."

"We'll do our best," Peter promised.

"I want you to remember, always, the chemistry that drew a couple together while not forsaking the work you still need to do."

"We'll remember, won't we Claire."

She nodded, agreeing.

"Now, I must leave you. Please enjoy your last evening on Daydream Island. You'll return here at 6:00 p.m. to share an intimate dinner for two."

Claire placed her palm on her cheek. "Sounds dreamy and romantic."

"I can't wait," Peter said, smiling.

Caroline stood. "I must be off. I'm returning to the main camp, but may I make a suggestion before I leave?"

"Of course," Claire replied.

"Take a walk on the beach. It's a beautiful day for a stroll."

"Maybe a swim, too." Peter said.

Claire suddenly felt impulsive. "Maybe we could jump off the dock like we used to."

Peter laughed. "Hand in hand? You're on!"

CHAPTER EIGHTEEN

*I*f Claire were honest with herself, this year's retreat had meant more to her than words could ever hope to express. She was overwhelmed with gratitude, grateful to friends and family for their support, and to Peter for being willing to build a new relationship by taking the counselling journey with her. Though it made traveling home more difficult. Could they manage the future, utilizing the advice they'd been given? What if circumstances didn't play out in the way they hoped?

In this new relationship, they had to build a new foundation, no different than the foundation of the Leonardo Bridge. What if they took a wrong step?

Their relationship was soon put through its paces. Monday morning arrived with her alarm ringing at five a.m., bringing her to alertness. She begrudgingly reached for the alarm and shut it off, not wanting to awaken Peter.

She rolled over, pulled on the sheets, and studied him in the bed. She touched his skin, feeling his warmth where he lay beside her. Peter had come home and his vibrancy, his voice and his presence, gave their home new meaning and new life. Laughter and conversation.

How could she leave him to go to work?

Claire didn't want to leave him, not to go to work, but the bakery needed her, pies and other bakery items required preparation, pie crusts and fillings, cinnamon buns and bread. All of this for their customers. In her life, consumers had played a significant role. No customers equaled an empty cash register. But what mattered most couldn't be found at a job.

The foundation built at retreat shook. She felt the vibration. It was too soon to spend time apart. It didn't feel right. His work, her work, had caused problems in their marriage. How did they negotiate a better future?

"Darn it," she muttered, climbing from the bed. She leaned over and kissed Peter on the cheek, lingering against his face. He muttered a nonsensical phrase in his sleep. She left the bedside, showered and dressed. She thought her heart would break in two while exiting the garage and driving along the road. Halfway to the bakery, the need to talk to her mom about hiring Nora became obvious. If their family friend was still interested in the position, the decision whether to hire Nora or not, should happen today.

CLAIRE WAS MIXING piecrust when the front door of the bakery opened. It wasn't even 7:00 a.m. What encouraged her mom to come to work so early? But it wasn't her mother who came around the corner and into the back room.

"Peter?" Claire shut off the mixer. "Why are you here?"

"You left without saying goodbye."

"I didn't want to wake you." She hadn't wanted to leave him either, but she left that part unsaid. "But I did kiss you."

"Wake me up before you leave, honey. I want to say good morning and goodnight each day for the rest of our lives."

Claire switched the mixer back on, a smile brightening her face. So happy to see him. "Is that why you're here, to say good morning?"

Peter reached for her mother's apron and tied it around his waist. Claire's eyes widened with surprise. She laughed. "What are you doing?"

"Putting on an apron. I don't think I've made a pie before. I'd like to learn."

"Are you kidding me, Peter Douglas?"

"When I woke up and you were gone, I could have stayed in bed and stared at the walls. I could have acted in a similar manner, traveling to my own place of business. I want my wife. I want to work on our foundation. Show me how to make a piecrust."

Claire grinned. She couldn't believe he had come to the family-owned bakery, let alone that he wanted to assist her with her pastry skills. She'd accept his help. She fastened his apron for him, not missing this opportunity to give him a hug. "You can start by washing your hands."

Peter went to the sink and massaged the soap in his hands. He looked silly in her mother's apron, but she wouldn't acknowledge it. She tried not to laugh but couldn't contain a giggle. When he looked at her, he smiled, accepting the humor.

"If you don't like my fashion statement, you'll have to get me my own apron. I'll be here at least once a week."

"You're planning on making this a permanent arrangement?" Claire stopped laughing. His comment surprised her.

"No. I'm lonely without you, and I thought if I helped, we could spend the day together."

"Share our first adventure?"

"A Monday morning date. We could go for a drive, go for a coffee, maybe take a walk on the beach."

Claire switched off the mixer and separated the dough into twelve balls, then passed a rolling pin to Peter. "You've watched me rolling pastry dough in the past. I begin by preparing the surface, ensuring it's clean, then coat the surface with flour, so the pastry won't stick to the countertop. Cleanliness is vital in food preparation. Then it's time to mold the pastry into a roundish circle prior to rolling."

"I might need help with the rolling. You might need to come closer."

Claire shook her head, enjoying the suggestion, then guided Peter. He followed her example. When they completed rolling the dough, it wasn't exactly flat, it wasn't perfect either, but Claire had never wanted perfection in her work or her relationship. She'd only ever wanted a spouse who would love her.

"Well done, Peter. Mom would be proud of you, shaping your own dough."

"It's not money," he said, rolling, "but it does feel good

creating something with my hands. Is that what it feels like to you when you're at work? Do you enjoy it? Is it worthwhile?"

She glanced at Peter, pausing with her rolling. "I don't like the early hours, but it does give me a sense of pride, continuing the family tradition."

Peter nodded. "It's too bad Stephanie and Christopher didn't come into the business. Maybe we made a mistake encouraging them to follow their own dreams."

"Maybe," Claire said, feeling wistful, wondering what would happen to the business in the future. They worked together until twelve pie shells were completed.

"What's next?" Peter asked.

"The filling."

"Claire, can we make key lime pie? I'm craving it."

Claire opened the fridge and saw prepared key lime filling. She smirked, thinking of her mother. "It looks like your craving will be satisfied. Did you talk to Mom? There's filling in the fridge."

"I might have told her I was coming by today."

He closed the fridge door and touched her nose, seemingly wiping a spot of flour off her face. Then he kissed her. And in her perception, there was nothing sexier than a man wearing an apron, even if it belonged to her mother. Baking pies relegated to a less important place while embracing Peter's broad shoulders. Urging him closer, she smothered him with kisses.

"Good morning, you two."

When Claire realized her parents had entered the workroom, she edged away from Peter but didn't leave his arms. "Mom? Dad? Why are you here so early?"

Her dad glanced at them in an amused manner. "Peter, why are you wearing Mary's apron?"

Peter chuckled and shifted closer to her side, pulling her into a hug. "I noticed there's not many masculine aprons in this family-owned bakery. Maybe we should make some changes, Burt."

"We'll definitely be making changes. I'm returning to work."

"What?" Claire said with a surprised tone. "Dad, you're retired."

"Not any longer, daughter. I was bored as heck at home. Now, don't get me wrong, there's nothing wrong with watching daytime soap operas, but I missed Mary. Never mind that I wasn't getting enough exercise. Mary and I have come to a decision."

Claire left Peter's embrace to retrieve fruit fillings from the fridge. "What have you decided?"

Mary touched Burt's arm. "Your father's a little excited. Look, we appreciate the changes you've made to the bakery, but in helping your parents have a better life, the business has hurt something far more important to us. Our kids."

"Hey, that's not fair," Peter said. He helped Claire retrieve more fillings from the fridge. "Claire and I can't blame the business operations for our problems. We need to handle our issues. I…need to make better choices."

"Peter's right. Mom, Dad, we should hire Nora. I wanted to talk to you about this."

"She's cute and she comes from a good family," Burt said.

Mary nudged Burt in the ribs. "What does beauty have to do with baking pies?"

"A pretty face behind the cash register is good for sales."

"Okay, Dad, but Nora might not want to live behind the cash register. Nora likes to bake and likely has other ambitions, too."

"I sure do," a new voice chimed in and Claire stood there, astonished, when Nora herself came around the corner and faced them, hands on her hips.

"I know this comes as a surprise, but Burt and I decided to hire Nora," Mary said, smiling. "We didn't talk about this prior to hiring Nora, so I hope it's okay, Claire. We don't want to upset you."

"Mom. Dad…I'm grateful you made this decision. Thank you for doing this." Claire left Peter's arms and give her parents a hug, then said to Nora, "Welcome to the bakery." She extended her hand. "I'm grateful you've agreed to work for us."

Nora reached into a bag and pulled out an apron. "Don't thank me yet. I have some new ideas for recipes, perhaps a few changes as well, so I hope you're receptive to change."

"Oh?" Claire murmured, suddenly not sure of this idea.

Nora tied her apron around her waist, confidence and enthusiasm in her expression. Come what may, that's when Claire decided to accept change. "I can't wait to hear your ideas."

Nora grasped the key lime pie filling. "We won't move too fast. Let's begin with the ingredients that your Old Thyme customers have come to enjoy. I hear one particular hero has his favorite."

"I have more to accomplish to earn that title." Peter

pulled Claire nearer to him. "But I'm as excited as the family to have you here."

"Thank you for the warm welcome."

"Claire and I, we have an adventure ahead of us. Five people cooking in the kitchen equals a lot of elbows banging against each other."

"Quitting so soon?" Claire asked, giggling. "Just when I got used to seeing you in an apron."

"We'll make sure we return in time for key lime pie."

CHAPTER NINETEEN

laire listened to the purr of Peter's SUV as they drove along the highway. As they left Ocean Park, she studied trees and bushes that lined either side of the road, while passing varying vehicles traveling south. She peered at Peter periodically, reflecting on his relaxed posture, his calm expression, the noticeable emotion in his eyes more so than the space between them. A strip of leather seat. She minded the gap, but as if Peter recognized her need to sit beside him, he patted the bench seat.

"Come on, slide over, sit beside me."

Claire didn't take the time to consider they were in a vehicle and traveling at highway speeds. Unfastening her safety belt, she shifted nearer to him. "Where are you taking me?" she asked, refastening her safety belt.

Peter glanced at her momentarily, his hands on the steering wheel. "To the place where we first met. I brought your bathing suit, a towel, and a hastily prepared lunch."

"Really? The ocean, the beach? It's the perfect day for a walk beside the water. Not too hot, not too cold." And she'd be walking beside Peter, which made it all the better. "It's a good afternoon for it," Claire said, recalling Sunset Beach. "It's a weekday, so hopefully it won't be crowded."

A pleasant shoreline, a couple could walk for miles on its silty sand. A girl with a family-owned bakery had responsibilities. The beach was her favorite place to escape life in the summer months, and she'd spend a lot of time there. Her body and soul uninhibited and free. Bare feet trekking across sand or wading into the water for a distance, not minding the coldness nipping at her skin, and no other worry other than the water reaching higher than a woman's waist. Sunset Beach was a popular place for sunbathing or exercise or catching the eye of a guy or two. She glanced at Peter, recalling the moment she'd caught his.

"Do you remember the last time we went to Sunset Beach?" Claire asked.

"As a couple? No, I don't," Peter said, seeming reflective. "Tells me it's been too long."

"How sad is that. To have a beautiful ocean so close to us and not taking the time to enjoy it. Peter, I wish…"

"What do you wish for? Tell me."

Claire thought about it. What did she want? "If we had financial freedom, if we could afford to take more time off…"

"We could start new and sell the house. Purchase a swanky singles pad for the two of us."

Claire grinned, picturing it. A tiny beach house nestled inside a cove near the ocean. She'd always wanted a breezeway, a porch where she could store pieces of driftwood and a bucket for shells. "I'd love to live near the water," she said, picturing it. "I'd walk on the beach every day."

Peter placed his hand on her knee. "We could consider it, but it would mean living farther away from Ocean Park, a longer drive to the bakery."

Claire frowned. The mention of the bakery gave her images of work. She didn't want responsibility to interfere with their day. "What do you want from the future? Are you serious, could you sell our house, the place where we raised our family?"

"Our home is lived in and comfortable, but I can't escape the fact that your eyes light up, simply from the idea of living near the ocean. Maybe we should consider it. A place by the sea or our existing home on a quiet, quaint street. Wherever we live, a home wouldn't be a home without you."

Claire pushed the dream away. "Maybe the timing isn't right."

"Maybe it's time to put us first. Take what *we* want from life."

"How do you think Stephanie and Chris would feel if their parents sold their family home?"

"We'll ask them, but they're busy with their own lives. We need to experience our life, too."

PETER HAD HIDDEN something from her. Now that Claire stood in a bathroom cubicle, she understood what the secret might be. She'd found her old yellow bikini in the carry bag. Did Peter expect her to wear this itsy-bitsy thing? Where had he found it? The swimsuit hadn't been worn in years, likely not since she was a teenager or a young wife. Hadn't she surrendered the garment to a secondhand store?

Reluctantly, Claire stepped into the bottoms, which were too tight. If she moved the wrong way the fabric would roll over her stomach. A ghastly feeling. The bikini top on the other hand molded to her boobs in an uncomfortable and awkward way, squishing them together. Her skin bulged between the folds. She couldn't leave the cubicle dressed like this. Everyone would stare at her, point at her, likely make fun of her, too.

Why, Peter? She silently moaned. When she discovered a white t-shirt at the bottom of a drawstring bag, she put it on, then placed a pair of white sandals on her feet. She left the change room, feeling uncomfortable. She didn't dare move in the wrong way.

Peter waited for her outside. She was ready to complain about the bathing suit, but paused, recognizing the wistful expression on his face. He was grinning from ear to ear. Why? She must look terrible.

She shook her head, not sure if she should laugh or cry. "Where'd you find this old thing? I thought I'd given it away."

Peter came forward, looking at her as if she were eighteen years old again. "Years ago, you asked me to take a bag of clothing to the secondhand store. I saw your old suit on the top."

"You retrieved it?"

"I held the fabric in my hand. I remembered seeing you for the first time, wearing this suit. I guess…I couldn't part with the memory any more than I could part with the bathing suit. I didn't want to embarrass you by letting you know I had kept it, so I hid it in my underwear drawer."

Claire felt uncomfortable. "You're embarrassing me. People are looking at me."

In truth, there were not that many beachgoers in the vicinity, but one couple walking past, younger and in better shape, made Claire self-critical of herself

"I know it doesn't fit you," Peter said, frowning. "I knew you might not be comfortable wearing it, which is why I included the t-shirt."

Claire shook her head. "News for you, it still doesn't fit me, and the suit's still visible beneath the shirt."

"Hear me out." He came forward and grasped her hand. "I've had the suit in my possession for years. Honey, I wanted to see my wife in this yellow suit again, to take me back to that first moment. I wanted to relive it. It's why I brought you to the beach."

He looked at her in a compelling way. A meaningful way. The discomfort receded, replaced by the realization that this moment was important to him, which meant it was important to her as well.

"Why is this scrap of fabric important?" Claire asked, forgetting the few people who walked past. "My body has changed. My clothing style has changed. A woman my age shouldn't stuff herself into a bikini."

Her protest didn't matter to him. Peter studied her as if

she were a model. "A woman your age? Honey, you can wear anything you want. You're gorgeous." He pulled her closer, squeezing her fingers. "I know it's a bit tight, but you look like a million dollars wearing it. Be still my heart, lest I have a heart attack."

Claire studied the wonderment in Peter's eyes. Her discomfort melted away, her worry of being seen in public, wearing a skimpy bathing suit, didn't matter. Peter admired her as if she were the most beautiful woman in the world. One itsy bitsy yellow bikini had only enhanced his view.

She smiled, astonished. "A lot has changed since that moment. Peter, I feel like the girl from the song, *Yellow Polka Dot Bikini*, who was afraid to come out of the locker."

Peter's expression brightened into a slight smile. "Things do seem constrictive. I bet you're glad I included the t-shirt."

Claire's right boob popped out of the bikini top. She tried not to cry out in mortification, as the look on Peter's face, the laughter he expressed simply from viewing her in old clothing that brought him joy, helped her to relax. She broke out in crazy laughter and passed him the bag, forcing her breast back inside the bikini top.

"Our visit to our favorite beach might be shorter than you planned," she said, grateful for the t-shirt.

Peter reached for her hand and she entwined her fingers within his. "Let me tell you something, I know there's an ocean view, blue water from here to the horizon, but I'll have a difficult time paying attention to anything other than you."

"Peter Douglas, you're full of surprises, and that's only one of the reasons why I love you."

They strolled alongside a boardwalk and soon passed a few

wooden stairs to the beach. Peter glanced at her frequently while walking on the shoreline. A wave of water sloshed across their feet and Claire tried to relinquish the awkward feeling to enjoy their time together.

She glanced at Peter's trunks. "I don't recall you wearing those bad boys the first time we met."

Peter chuckled, squeezing her fingers. "I gave those board shorts away a long time ago."

Claire shook her head, laughing. "Of course you did, but you let me wear this old thing?"

"From my point of view, you look better than the ocean."

Claire paused, realizing her worst fear had come to pass. She reached for her bikini top underneath the white t-shirt.

"What's wrong?" Peter asked.

"My fastener broke. What do I do, Peter?"

"Live your life, be free, and get comfortable."

Claire removed the bikini top and passed it into his hand, feeling uncomfortable and free at the same time. She didn't know what made her happier, freedom from the restriction, or having the free will to act however she pleased.

Peter winked at her. "I see what you're thinking, but the suit's going back in my drawer."

"If it means that much to you, who am I to steal the memories, but I think it's time for new ones. Maybe I can convince the girls to go shopping with me before they leave. I suppose you'd support a yellow suit?"

"Anything that puts a smile on your face, Claire." His expression softened. Not from an ocean breeze or even the sun. Love brightened his eyes.

Claire kept calm and carried on. She held his hand as they

walked along the beach. Laughter rang in the air. Sweet memories affected them from the past. And an itsy bitsy, teeny weeny, yellow bathing suit clutched inside Peter's hand made her feel freer than she had ever felt before.

Some memories were better than others, and she'd always be grateful for meeting this man.

Peter Douglas, a huge smile painted on his face, loved her, despite saggy breasts beneath a white t-shirt and wrinkles at the corner of her eyes.

"I'll race you to the dock," she said, giggling.

Claire kicked off her sandals and Peter dropped the bag he'd been carrying. When they reached the end of the dock, perched on its end, Peter asked her, "Are you sure?"

"I've never been surer of anything. Jump!"

And they did, together.

The water chilled her, enveloped her, causing shivers. And then Peter swam toward her. They moved toward a shallower spot and then stood, embracing each other. Her hair wet, water dripping down her face and into her eyes.

Seeming emotional, Peter clutched her head. The look in his eyes almost undid her. "You're beautiful…"

"Kiss me, Peter."

Everything stopped: sounds of conversation, other people splashing in the water. The world probably stopped spinning when he kissed her. "My god, I love you," he said, lifting her in the water. She wrapped her legs around his waist, clinging to him. "I want to love you, each and every day for the rest of my life. I don't want distance to *ever* come between us again."

Claire clutched his face, water escaping her eyes, more

tears than ocean. "I love you, too. My heart couldn't go on without you beside me."

They left the water and trudged toward shore, soon wrapping themselves in towels. Neither Claire nor Peter wanted to leave the beach. It was clear to them, this ocean playground helped them find their happy place.

CHAPTER TWENTY

The team met early the next morning at the Railway Café to discuss the bakery and its future. New people encouraged new ideas, and Nora seemed excited to share her ideas. Claire tried to listen to the conversation but found it difficult engaging, never mind hearing the brief snippets of dialogue. The previous day's events had her staring beyond the café's booth, looking through the window at the clouds.

Her mother, sitting across from her, snapped her fingers. "Claire, you're being rude. Nora is speaking."

Claire looked at Nora. "I'm sorry. I've had changes in my personal life recently. I know that doesn't excuse my inattention. I'll will be more present in this conversation."

Nora's eyebrows rose, expressing her curiosity. "My mama always said if my thoughts were so important that they took my attention away from an important conversation, then I had to share what was on my mind so I wouldn't lose focus again. It's probably the encouragement I needed to inspire ambition. If you don't mind, what's going on?"

Claire hadn't anticipated an awkward moment, but her awareness drifted to changes in her life. Her relationship with Peter had begun again and she had much to consider, but this didn't excuse her for being rude to Nora. "If I get started, I don't know if I'll be able to stop."

Burt slid out from the booth. "This is a good time to take a break. I'll be right back, ladies."

"Out with it," Nora said, grinning. "We're friends; I don't gossip. You can trust me when I say the thoughts burning a hole in your mind will not be repeated. Think of it as an icebreaker or a friendship maker."

"You'll think this is silly, but I was thinking about Peter," Claire said wistfully. "I'm in love."

"It's not what I thought you'd say, but you smiled so sweetly while saying your husband's name. How many years have you been married?"

"Our anniversary is coming on July 1st. We've been married for nearly twenty-six years."

"Congratulations. Many couples don't last five years let alone twenty-five."

"Well," Claire said, glancing at her mom, "we've had a few problems in our relationship recently, but thanks to the support of family and friends, our marriage has managed to survive. It's better than ever."

"I'm happy for you. Now with your joy out in the open, maybe we can talk about the future of Old Thyme Bakery?"

"I promise to pay better attention to your ideas."

Burt returned to his seat. "Ready to talk business, ladies?"

"Yes," the team replied enthusiastically.

Nora opened a journal and reached for a pen. "I've asked you here because I'm excited to work with you. What I'm about to say might be surprising. I have a business proposition, so please hear me out."

"You have the floor," Burt replied, "what do you have in mind?"

Nora took her time to address each of them, staring them down, as if what she had to share was important. That look garnered Claire's curiosity.

"In a society where name brands take market share of customers, there's not enough support for unique businesses, family-owned businesses, such as your bakery."

"I agree with you," Burt commented. "I mean, name brands have their place, but in a small town like Ocean Park, 'supporting local' businesses fuels the town economy. Is that what you meant to say, Nora?"

"To be honest, I want to invest in the bakery. I'd like to own twenty-five to fifty percent of the business."

Complete silence. An awkward pause. Claire searched her parents' expressions, wondering what this pitch meant to them. When they'd agreed to a staff meeting, they had expected to engage in conversation with a new employee. Taking on a business partner came as a surprise.

"We're flattered that you find value in the bakery," Claire said, glancing at her parents. "But I'm surprised. I had expected to talk about daily happenings, such as pastry assortments, pies, bread, that sort of thing."

"Claire, I'm fired up with ideas. Partly due to my mother for teaching me to never hold back on my ideas. If you'd hear me out, we could expand the bakery, its product line, and if you're open to the idea, maybe talk about changing the name to the Old Thyme Café?"

"Change the name?" Burt shook his head, fingering his mug of coffee. "I don't know. I'm fond of the name. But if we were open to selling you a share in the company, our current space would be too small for an eatery."

"We could leave the names as is, break down the wall, and take over the space next door. The Old Thyme Bakery and the Old Thyme Café?"

"I don't know," Burt said, taking a sip of coffee, "sounds like a lot of work."

"My husband would help. He's handy with a hammer and he's a chef by trade. We've been searching for a business to invest in and want to support a known place."

Claire appealed to her parents. "What do you think, mom and dad? Do you want to sell a portion of your business? As before we can consider growing the company, we'd have to consider if Nora's idea has merit."

"The question is yours to answer as this business is your inheritance," Mary said, glancing at Burt. "Claire, how do you feel about a partner?"

She opened her mouth to speak but then didn't know what to say. This was sudden. How did she feel? "I'm honestly not sure."

Burt added his own opinion. "We should give Nora's offer serious consideration. If we hold on too tight to the bakery, we'll break it. We'll lose it. The bakery has been difficult to manage on our own. Claire, honestly, the bakery almost destroyed your marriage."

Her father's admission came as a surprise to Nora. Claire had to set the record straight. "It's not the business's fault. Time management is the issue."

Burt drummed his fingers on the table. "Claire, what happens when Mary and I can't work anymore, can't help anymore, what then? The responsibility becomes yours again." Her father addressed Nora. "Let's say we're agreeable to taking you on as a partner. We know you're a dedicated professional who will manage the bakery in an appropriate way. But are there other ideas you could share with us?"

"Well, initially I thought one large space where two businesses could function as one entity, but maybe that's the wrong concept. Maybe there should be two businesses operating independently, but together, too. A bakery and a café with a pass-through doorway in between. You'd carry the sundry and pastry items that you're known for, like pies, but we'd increase the assortment with lunch options and maybe entrées at dinner."

"I wish our breakfast would arrive," Burt said. "I'm suddenly hungry."

"We'd take care of breakfast in the café, too."

"I'm not saying I'm open to the idea, but if we're to give serious thought to your offer, how could we be different?" Claire asked.

"You could start by using varying ingredients, maybe provide vegan options, gluten-free, and maybe low-carb foods suitable for ketogenic diets."

Claire tapped her finger against her mug, giving serious consideration to Nora's concept. It excited her to mull over a bakery/café. Pictures took shape in her mind. A soup kitchen paired with scones. Panini sandwiches using the bakery's fresh bread.

"You've thought this through. I love the idea of having a variety of items. A café sounds exciting and could bring new life to the bakery," Claire said.

"I like the concept as well." Mary nodded. "Nora, what do you think about one name: The Old Thyme Bakery and Café? Would that be agreeable to you?"

"We began this conversation talking about the importance of local establishments," Nora said, looking at them seriously. "So yes, adding on café to an already perfect name is doable."

Claire giggled. "It's so simple. Recognizable, but also new."

"We need to evaluate the company's worth," Burt said, glancing at Mary and then at Claire. "We'll also need to find out how much we'll need to invest to bring a café into the business." Even though her father seemed excited, he paused. Did he have reservations? "Ladies, are you in favor of pursuing this?"

Claire searched her parents' expressions then looked at Nora. "Yes, I am. Nora, your business proposal sounds like a solid idea. I'm excited about pursuing it."

"I'm glad to hear it," Nora said. "Just one more question. The bakery has always been a family-owned business. Does it bother you that you're considering growing the business with two partners who aren't family?"

"Why should it?" Claire asked.

"If it's a concern of yours, we could always adopt you." Burt said with a laugh.

Nora's expression took on one of relief. "Thank you. I was nervous. I didn't expect such a positive response."

"We have a lot to work out, but your timing couldn't be more perfect. Let's have a toast." Claire lifted her coffee, and her parents and Nora did the same. "To the future."

CHAPTER TWENTY-ONE

When Nora presented her business proposal, it had seemed like a good idea, but now Claire wasn't certain. By the look on Peter's face, he didn't like the idea.

"What did you say?" he asked.

Claire slumped onto the sofa in their family room, wondering if a mistake had been made. "Nora offered to purchase a portion of the bakery, a twenty-five to fifty percent share in the business. I hesitated at first but having Nora as a business partner could lessen my responsibilities."

"Maybe in the kitchen. Help me with the math. How do you lessen responsibilities when you're adding a café to an already heavy workload?"

Claire sighed. Peter made a valid comment. Acknowledging this caused doubt to spring to the surface, increasing her anxiety. Had she made a mistake in being excited about the prospect of a partner? Maybe she should have thought it over more.

"You're right. You have legitimate concerns."

"Don't get me wrong, I don't want to diminish your excitement. I can see how much you love this idea."

"It's true. I am excited, but I understand why you might not agree with me," Claire said, realizing Peter recognized the potential issues, which wasn't surprising given he worked as an accountant. "You've always been smarter with numbers than me."

"I didn't mean to suggest that you lacked intelligence. You're a brilliant woman, Claire. Let's talk about the proposal reasonably as I honestly feel blindsided."

Claire took a deep breath, trying to remain calm. "I know this comes as a surprise, but it's new to me as well. I had no idea the bakery had caught Nora's interest."

Peter sat on the couch. "I'm all in favor of the assistance, even a partner that isn't family. Though I'm concerned it could increase your workload."

"We're talking in circles. Nothing has been decided. But keep in mind that Nora's husband would be entering the business as well."

"That's great, I'm in favor of that part. I'm mostly concerned about us. The timing is part of the problem. We're working on our marriage."

"All right, so here we are, facing our first test. This won't be the first or last time that situations arise. Let's think of this point, too. Nora's husband is a chef, but now that I think about it…"

"…you're starting to see that increased square footage equals more work. Look, if the idea is to freshen the family brand and increase customers, it's probably a great idea. I'm most worried about how it will affect us."

Claire made to rise, but Peter grasped her hand. "We can't avoid this conversation. Sit beside me, Claire. Let's talk this through." He squeezed her hand. "It's okay. I'm not upset with you."

Claire heaved an exasperated breath. "We've only begun discussions, but I would assume that my role would continue to focus on the bakery side of things, and if that's the case, my workload wouldn't change much."

"This is the early stages, so I'm sure there's a lot to reason through; I just don't want my wife working more hours."

"We're putting our lives back together. We're spending more time together," Claire said. She looked at Peter, exasperated, seeing the unease in his expression. Worry consumed her, too. "Peter, I supported Mom and Dad in this. They were excited about the opportunity; however, I see your concern and you're right to ask questions. I can't permit space to come between us again. What do I do?"

He massaged her knee, his expression softening into a half-smile. "Why are your parents excited?" His tone gave her a more optimistic impression. His look compelled her to continue.

Claire slid her hand through her hair, trying to explain. "While the bakery is a family-owned business, our kids have shown no interest in coming on board, so if someone else purchases a share, the family legacy continues."

"Maybe. There's no guarantees. Taking on a partner will add risk."

Claire studied his face, searching his expression, not

knowing what to do. "Should I talk to Mom and Dad? Tell them we should rethink this idea?"

"No. I want to know about my wife's expectations. Tell me what you want. Do you want to expand the bakery?"

"Maybe, but not if you don't support the concept. Peter, right now, I'm most afraid that we'll slide backwards, or fail. I couldn't bear it if we fell apart again."

"It's not happening. Not today. Not ever." He embraced her cheek and she leaned into his warmth. "Somehow, it has to get easier."

Claire nodded, feeling supported.

"I tell you what, why don't I crunch some numbers for you. For your parents. Evaluate the company's net worth and consider what an expansion might cost."

"What does that mean? Do you support the idea?"

His thumb massaged her cheek. She loved the sensation.

"I'm supporting my wife," Peter said, nodding. "Don't worry, Claire. If you want to pursue a business relationship with Nora, if you're excited about Nora's concept, then let's see if it's doable. I'm on your side. I want to see you smile."

"Do you mean it?"

"Yes, I do. I trust your instincts. You're right. Maybe it is a good idea to have someone else who cares about the bakery as much as you."

"Why are you agreeing to this?"

"A man shouldn't hold his wife back. A man should believe in his wife."

"Will you kiss me, Peter?"

"I thought you'd never ask."

CHAPTER TWENTY-TWO

A husband must bear the responsibility in protecting his wife and his marriage. Other couples might see their obligations differently, but Peter's opinion seemed stronger than ever on the subject given recent tribulations. He'd failed Claire by retreating from their relationship, and he wasn't about to build barriers that might compromise their relationship a second time.

He had an idea. A meaningful concept, and his father-in-law was the best person to share potential goals.

They'd agreed to meet at the local bar. A country honky-tonk with wood-plank floors, a massive oval bar top, and a juke box machine. Father and son-in-law had chosen to sit at stools at the bar rather than a table. Peter listened to Garth Brooks singing about rolling thunder while a server placed two beers in front of them. "Thanks for meeting me, Burt."

His father-in-law massaged the beer bottle with his fingers, looking at him in a knowing way. "I suspect this visit

157

isn't simply to shoot the breeze. Claire must have told you about the business offer."

"Yes, she did," Peter said with a frown. "The news surprised me."

Burt took a slug of his beer. "If you think we jumped on the bandwagon and went to town with the idea, that's not the way it played out. Mary and I were as surprised as you. Peter, old folks like us, it's difficult to accept change at the best of times and taking on a partner, well…that's a *big* change."

"I didn't mean to imply that you rushed into the decision. You're one of the smartest men I know."

"Aw heck, I'm not offended. I appreciate the gesture, but Mary and I have been living our life in a simple way for many years, which makes us hesitant to accept such an offer, but the more we consider Nora's offer, the more excited we get. How do you feel about it?" Burt asked, taking a sip of his beer.

How did he feel? If Peter were honest, the business offer concerned him. Restaurants failed, and the family business wasn't a money-making enterprise in its current form, however, he must come to terms with his doubt. Guilt consumed him for not supporting Claire. They needed to rectify the situation. "I didn't respond in the way Claire hoped. I might have sunk her excitement."

Burt shook his head, chuckling. "I bet the numbers guy went straight to his calculator and punched buttons."

"Something like that," Peter said, shaking his head. "I apologize if I've offended you."

"Hey, you're an accountant, I wouldn't expect anything less from you. One of the members of this family has to consider the potential for profit and loss."

"Burt, that's not it at all. I don't want you to get the wrong idea that I'm not supportive."

"Peter, it's not like you to be down in the dumps. Whatever's bothering you, let it out. I know we're not at this honky-tonk to have a beer. Tell me what's on your mind. I can't help if you don't tell me what's wrong."

Peter took a sip of his beer, then studied Burt's concerned expression. "You're right, I do feel burdened, but my worries have nothing to do with the bakery. I've been mulling over an idea myself, which has nothing to do with the business, but I have not spoken about it to Claire."

Claire would never agree to the idea. Keeping secrets was wrong. Peter knew this. But sacrifices on his part must be made to better their future together.

"I've been told a time or two that I'm good at giving advice. After all the years we've known each other, you should know by now you can confide anything to me."

Peter took a second sip of his beer. He listened to country music playing, the buzz of conversation stirring in the air around him. It didn't matter how old one became, the decisions in one's life didn't get easier. Change was difficult for young and old alike. "Burt, I'm considering selling the accounting firm."

The revelation seemed to surprise Burt. His face wrinkled with concern. "Why would you do that?"

"After I explain, I think you'll understand. The way I see it, two businesses plus two partners equals too many complications, such as Claire and me working too much. I'm worried we'll lose focus in our marriage and end up right back where we started. In trouble. I don't see another path forward."

"Peter, you don't have to give up your business."

Peter raised his hand. "Just listen…I can't ask Claire to walk away from a family business. It's too important to her."

"Why would she have to? Help me understand."

"We're trying to make changes in our marriage."

"I know. You've been working hard. Claire certainly seems happier. Peter, there hasn't been enough time to think things through."

"I've thought about it, every day and every night. Selling the accounting firm seems like the best option."

"Claire wouldn't expect you to make such a sacrifice."

"No, of course not," Peter said, pausing. He stared at other people in the bar, happy people, some couples dancing; he never wanted to lose that joy. "We're two people pursuing two businesses, the work is complicating our life. It might be better if there was only one business."

Burt's eyes rose with interest. "Peter Douglas, what are you suggesting?"

"I trust you, Burt. If you'll have me, I want to be a partner in the Old Thyme Bakery and Café. I'd sell my business, invest in the new concept, and ensure my marriage remains healthy."

Burt took a swig of his beer, then placed his bottle on the bar top with a resounding thwack. "Well, I'll be damned," he said, shaking his head. "If someone had told me my son-in-law would be making pies at the bakery, I'd have told them they were crazy." His father-in-law had the audacity to roar with laughter.

Peter snickered, remembering his training session. "Claire showed me how to roll pastry dough. I'll do it if it makes her happy." Peter paused. Was he willing to go to such lengths? "Burt, am I crazy for having this idea, for making this proposal?"

Burt grasped his shoulder. "Son, I'd be proud to have you in the business, but you must consider the difficulties in a working relationship. Spending too much time with the one you love, day after day, well...that can cause complications, too."

"Is that why you retired?"

"All I'm saying is a couple needs space to balance the relationship."

"You're a smart man." Peter took a slug of his beer, thinking about Burt's point of view on the subject. "Claire and I have had too much space. She's excited about the expansion and I want to support the concept."

"Regardless of what I say, I see you're set on selling."

"Damn straight."

Burt's face lit up like he'd won the lotto. "I can't believe it. You've made an old man happy. Mary will be pleased, too. There's probably a greater chance of the bakery café concept being successful with you involved."

"I'm just a numbers guy. I'll have a lot to learn about the family business, but there will be six of us now. And no more complications with Claire. We can even travel back and forth from work together."

"When will you tell Claire?"

"When the time is right. She'll try and talk me out of the sale, and I want to do something meaningful for her."

"Something more than selling your business? That's a pretty significant step on its own."

Peter nodded, smiling, imagining how Claire would respond to his gift. He had a good idea that their twenty-sixth anniversary would be an amazing experience, if he could pull this off. Their anniversary was in two weeks. "You have no idea."

"Burt, there's one more idea I'd like to propose to you."

"Peter, you're grinning from ear to ear. What is it?"

"Just you wait."

CHAPTER TWENTY-THREE

Claire stood on her front doorstep, watching the FedEx truck leaving her home after delivering a parcel. While holding the small box in her hands, she scanned the address label, reading her name. Who had sent the package? She didn't recall placing an order. She shook the box, curious about the contents.

Reentering the house, she walked along the hallway toward the kitchen, where Peter sat at the table, drinking coffee, and reading news on his phone. "What do you have there?" he asked, gauging her expression.

"A package, but I don't recall placing an order."

"That's interesting. I wonder who sent it. You should open it, find out what's inside."

"All right."

Claire didn't concern herself with the intrigue surrounding the sender while retrieving a kitchen knife. Her curiosity focused on the contents of the package and the desire to identify the object inside. She took the package and the knife to the kitchen table, where she sat. The knife slid through edges of thick banded tape. She placed the knife on the tabletop and opened the lid.

"This box holds something beautiful. I can tell by the sticker and the extravagant wrapping." A gold Parisian sticker affixed to ivory tissue paper caught her attention. Claire glanced at Peter, who was grinning. After nearly twenty-six years of marriage, she recognized that look.

"Did you order this for me?"

"I may have." His grin spread wider. "Open it, Claire."

"What did you do?" she asked, holding the bulk in her hands. After retrieving the bundle from the box, she passed the cardboard to Peter. She carefully peeled away the sticker and folded back delicate layers. A yellow bathing suit...A bikini. "Peter, what is this?"

He dropped the box on the floor and got up from his chair. "What does it look like? A new memory to fit your womanly curves."

Claire held the bra top, fingering the fabric. The V-neck design had a band of ruffles beneath the bustline. "From Paris of all places? What a surprise. It's beautiful."

"The bottoms are high waisted," Peter said, coming closer, "and suitable for a curvy figure. I hope you'll be comfortable wearing them. Do you want to try the suit on; would you try it on, for your husband?"

"Oh...I don't know. I mean, I appreciate your thoughtfulness, but do you think it's appropriate for a forty-something wife to wear a skimpy bathing suit? People will look at my belly."

"I'll look at your belly," Peter said, winking.

"Furthermore, that suit is not skimpy. Honey, you might not be a size four anymore, but there's nothing wrong with your shape, or a healthy size twelve."

Claire was aghast that Peter knew her size. Every woman knew that weight and sizing were deeply held secrets. "How did you learn this piece of information?"

"It was more difficult than I thought it would be. I'm sorry to confess this, honey, but I searched through your drawers. A difficult pursuit, many of the clothing labels were unreadable. I should have bought you two suits instead of one."

Claire fingered the garment, appreciating the gesture. "This means a lot to me, Peter."

"I want to see you in that suit." He reached for her hand. "Will you try it on?"

Claire felt as timid as she had the day in the locker room. Peter's gift had taken her emotions to a delicate place. "I'll try it on," Claire said, grasping his hand. She permitted him to escort her to their bedroom, holding the bathing suit in her hands, then retreated to the ensuite to try on the bathing suit.

It molded to her figure, fitting her perfectly. She fingered the fabric, staring at herself in the mirror. *Am I beautiful?* She didn't look terrible wearing the suit. The band of ruffles beneath the bustline flattered the style. The yellow color was significant. It reminded her of the beginning of their relationship. Maybe this new suit represented their renewal.

Claire left the ensuite. Peter was sitting on their bed, waiting for her. His eyes lit up. He whistled. "Oh, honey, you look amazing. Do you like it? Are you happy with it? If you don't love it, if it doesn't bring you joy, I'll buy you another."

SHELLEY KASSIAN

Claire grasped her face, completely blindsided. "Peter, it's beautiful."

"Then why are you sad?"

Claire shifted her hands to her sides, standing in front of him, feeling old and awkward, and emotional. "You've caught me by surprise. And I…"

"And you what? Lay your burdens down."

"I don't know what to say. I mean, thank you. You've made me feel like the girl you married years ago. Somehow, you've reconnected me to my teenage heart."

"I suppose this means I should have spoiled you sooner," Peter said, rising from the bed. "But let me tell you, you are the woman I married years ago. And to look at you now, in your beautiful yellow bikini, I want you to overcome your *itsy-bitsy* worries and come over here and kiss me."

Claire took a deep breath, then released her nervous energy in a tentative giggle, but was soon held in his arms, grateful for his kisses, which only served to make her feel more loved than ever.

"I have another surprise. How would you like to go away for the weekend? Maybe take a drive up to Honeymoon Bay? Our anniversary is coming up, so considering that, I've taken the liberty of renting us a house on the bay. One of those Airbnb places."

"Will I get the chance to wear my suit?" Claire chuckled, a huge smile on her face.

"The house has a hot tub, and an amazing view of the ocean, even a private beach."

"It's sounds perfect. I can't wait." She'd go today if he asked her.

166

Peter laughed. He seemed happy as well. He walked to his closet and retrieved a shopping bag. "I want to share new memories with you."

"What do you have in your hands?" Claire asked, expressing her surprise.

"You'll need more than one bathing suit for what I have planned. You'll need a new dress in your wardrobe. On our anniversary, I want to take you to a restaurant in the hills, overlooking the ocean."

"Can we afford it, given the bakery expansion?"

"It's our anniversary. It only comes around once a year, and this year is special."

"You've thought of everything," Claire said. "I'm surprised, and grateful."

He came toward her and passed her the bag. "Let's have some more fun. I can't wait for the fashion show."

"I love you, Peter Douglas."

It was great fun, unwrapping his gifts. Claire appreciated the fact that not every item was yellow. After all, pinks and sexy reds were her favorite colors, and good for her complexion, too.

CHAPTER TWENTY-FOUR

*C*laire had difficulty focusing on her work the next day. Thoughts of Peter spurred on by the gifts he had given her, plus the excitement of an anniversary weekend, had her in a state of wonder. In all the years a husband and wife had been married, Peter had never shown her such attentiveness. He overflowed with courtesy, compassion, attending to her every need.

What had motivated the new focus in her life? The simple question, asking if she was okay. Her heart filled with joy. Life seemed different. Everything brighter, clearer. Even Peter had taken on new meaning. A fresh haircut, clean shaven and smelling like aftershave; he was more handsome than ever.

"Someone's happy," Nora said, creaming butter and sugar together.

Claire paused in her breadmaking to ponder her colleague's work, a woman who had quickly become a close friend and confidant. "You're a great addition to the team," Claire said, glancing at Nora. "I don't know which aspect of your experience I appreciate more, your skill as a baker or your ideas. We've made some exciting changes."

Nora reached for the flour and added several cups to a stainless steel bowl in a no-nonsense kind of way. "I'm grateful you accepted me as part of the team, not everyone adapts to change as well as you and your parents. Not everyone would permit an outsider as a partner in their business."

"You're not an outsider," Claire stated. "We were impressed by your approach, your ideas. And honestly, the company needed energy, a new focus and direction. We couldn't embrace the future without you."

"I thought Burt and Mary would say no. It occurred to me that seniors with an established business wouldn't accept a couple who were different. Never mind my outspokenness; I'm bold at times, a bit stern, too."

Claire turned on the bread machine and let the paddles work. "If it's acceptable, I'll put you in charge of the complaints department," Claire said with a giggle, "but seriously, while I love pies, expanding our assortment and putting the breakfast items and pastries out at different times of the day, varying days sometimes, that's a win for the bakery."

Nora added eggs, and then dry ingredients to the bowl. "In your view, have the changes been positive, have they increased customer traffic or contributed to the bottom line—the register?"

"Yes, to both. Word gets around quickly in a small town. I mean, who wants to eat pie at 8:00 a.m.? Personally, there's nothing better than raspberry chocolate scones with

Devonshire cream. And testing the various new items has given us a good indication if our customers will accept further change as well."

"They haven't had to adapt to much. The pies still come out, only later in the day."

"The pie and cupcake idea was brilliant," Claire said, "and it's been well received."

"The calories are substantial, but it's a delicious mix," Nora replied. "You must be excited that Peter supported the changes, especially the café concept."

Claire turned off the bread machine. "We haven't spoken much about the bakery since I told him about the offer. To be honest, adding on to the business concerned him."

"Well, you must have motivated a change. It's amazing that Peter and you will invest in the business as well. With the six of us supporting the bakery, the café will be successful."

"What? You have this wrong. Peter and I have had no such conversation."

"Maybe I'm mistaken, but I'm certain Burt told Jim that we wouldn't be the only investors."

Claire stared at Nora, her voiced sentiment causing shock waves to roll through her mind. Was it true? Peter investing in the bakery... It couldn't possibly be real. He hadn't been supportive of the café, even so, he had been full of surprises lately. Claire didn't know what to believe.

"Nora, please be honest with me, is it true? Has Peter invested in the bakery?"

"I see by your stunned expression that you didn't know." Nora paused with her work. "I apologize for spoiling the secret. Claire, there must be a good reason that he hasn't told you."

Claire stared at the mixer, taken aback. "Never mind Peter, my parents have not told me."

"And there's likely a good reason for their secrecy."

Secrecy. She didn't like secrets and didn't know how to feel about this one. "Why wouldn't they tell me?"

"Isn't it obvious, it must be a surprise."

"A surprise."

"Yes, and when Peter reveals the truth, you must promise to act surprised."

"Act surprised…"

"I'm sorry," Nora said with a frown. "I've spoiled everything."

Claire didn't say anything while spreading flour on the counter. The bread dough came next. She maneuvered it with her hands, rolling it and giving it a few good punches. "Why do men keep secrets? Why can't they tell the truth?"

"Who knows. A woman leads by example and a man thinks he has the answer for everything. Can I tell you what I know for sure?"

"Go ahead," Claire replied, reaching for a knife.

"From what you've told me, you came close to losing your marriage. Peter might be working too hard at making amends. It does seem like he's on a mission to ensure neither of you go through heartbreak again. The situation you find yourself in might surprise you, but don't be angry with Peter."

Claire portioned the dough into several pieces. "I'm not angry, I wish he had told me."

"Like I told you before, he probably wants to tell you in

his own way. I'm sure he means well. He's probably got a big party planned."

"The next thing you'll tell me is to pretend I don't know about the investment."

Nora smiled at her while preparing biscuit tins for her scones. "Exactly, and I know how difficult that will be."

Claire shook her head, continuing her work. But Nora was right. No different than the new bathing suit or the anniversary weekend, Peter strove to put her first in his life. She hoped he knew how much it meant to her that he soared toward change. Though material objects, even an investment in the bakery, didn't matter to her. All Claire needed was his love.

CHAPTER TWENTY-FIVE

The weather promised the perfect weekend for a couple retreating from their busy lives. Brilliant sunlight sparkled on the water. Not one cloud drifted in the sky. In the passenger seat of Peter's Volvo XC40, Claire scrutinized him, excited about the anniversary weekend.

The mini vacation came as a pleasant surprise. As they zoomed along the highway, Peter's right hand rested comfortably on the steering wheel. His posture exuded calm and happiness. He glanced her way and smiled. When he returned his attention to the road, she pondered their destination.

Peter hadn't divulged anything. Not even one clue.

He had worn his best casual clothes: a blue striped shirt lay open at his neck, distressed blue jeans shaped nicely to his hips and waist. The effort implied this weekend meant as much to him as it did to her. When he glanced at her again, offering a mischievous grin, Claire remembered the amusing boy she'd fallen in love with, yet his hidden truths still made her suspicious.

A question rolled round and round in her mind. When would he tell her about the intention to invest in the bakery? And did she have the patience to wait?

Peter winked at her as if he recognized her curiosity. Normally she'd nag at him to learn the truth, such as this drive toward an unknown destination. He'd hinted at Honeymoon Bay for their anniversary, but something seemed off, not only their direction of travel, but also his behavior. He acted differently, caring for her in an overcautious kind of way. After what they'd been through, it shouldn't surprise her, but Claire wondered if there was something more. Maybe Peter had a reason for his silence. Maybe she should respect his motives and wait for the big reveal. Yet waiting had never been her strong point. The hardest part, thanks to Nora, was knowing a portion of Peter's kept secret.

Claire glanced at a logging truck they were passing, trying to focus her attention on the anniversary weekend. Peter had been secretive about this, too. Still, it couldn't hurt to nudge him a little. She fingered his cotton shirt in a tempting, suggestive way. *If I give you something, will you give me something, too?*

"Where are you taking me, Peter?"

"Wouldn't you like to know," he replied, glancing at her. "I'd love to tell you, but do you *really* want me to spoil the surprise? You like surprises, don't you?"

"Depends on what it is," Claire said, amused by his enthusiasm. "This surprise is trying my patience. It's killing me. I'm dying to know where we're going."

"You don't like surprises?"

"I like the new clothing. Can't wait to wear that new dress."

"Chin up, love. Not knowing the destination might seem like I'm denying you, but think of it like this—I've put a lot of thought into our weekend. I want to enjoy three perfect days. I promise, you'll love it."

"This weekend is important to you."

"More than you know."

"You can't blame me for being curious," Claire said, stroking his waist. Her fingers slid underneath his cotton shirt; soft skin met her fingertips and teased him. "You have to give me a clue. How long will it take to reach our destination?"

"You don't play fair." Peter laughed, staring at the road ahead. "All right. It's a bit of a journey. It will take us approximately two hours to get there."

Claire considered the time frame, mentally calculating prime vacation spots. "It can't be Parksville, the city's not far enough. Perhaps we're travelling somewhere near Nanaimo? What about Deep Bay, Fanny Bay, or Denman Island?"

Peter touched her knee, appearing to enjoy the suspense. "Aren't you curious. I'll play your game. I'll release another clue. We're taking a boat across the Strait of Georgia."

"We're traveling by ferry?" Claire said excitedly.

"We're taking a water taxi from Ladysmith to a remote location, someplace special for my wife, and that's all you're getting from me. For now."

A ferry across the water. If it left from Ladysmith, their destination must be a more secluded, private location.

Maybe an island? The perfect place for desire and clandestine cares.

"Okay. I won't bother you for more answers."

"Great," Peter said, returning his attention to the roadway.

It wasn't long before they arrived at the harbor. Peter loaded her suitcase and his own into a 26-foot water taxi. The breeze threaded through her hair as he brought a third bag onboard. "What's inside your bag, Peter?"

"Wine," he said, smiling. "If you're lucky, your favorite artisanal cheeses."

"You've thought of everything."

The skookum boat's engine fired up. They were soon motoring across the water. Claire looked at Peter while listening to the boat's motor, feeling the ocean spatter against her face. The breeze causing her hair to fly. "Now will you tell me?" she asked, her tone jovial.

Peter touched her face, his fingers sliding through her hair. He grasped a wayward strand that flipped in the wind and tucked it behind her ear. "You forced it out of me. Ruxton Island, our private getaway for the weekend."

"I've never been to Ruxton Island. What should I expect?"

"Honey, I'm satisfying your every desire." He didn't speak for a moment as if suggesting all the ways he'd impart her pleasure. "I've booked a home with a spectacular view. We have a private boat launch. A quaint cove, and so much more. You can swim naked in the bay if you want."

"Ha, ha!" Claire tittered at the suggestion. "You say that as if you want me to take the chance. I don't think so, Peter. It wouldn't be appropriate."

"Makes you uncomfortable? What about sunbathing naked?" He looked at her hopefully, smiling.

Claire burst out laughing. "What has gotten into you? It's like I'm looking at a whole new man."

"I feel amazing; I feel alive," he replied, studying the wake behind the boat. "I'm happier than I've felt in months." He grasped her hand. "You're the reason for my happiness. I'm in love with my wife and I can't wait to reach the island and share the weekend with you."

In that moment, Claire felt loved, felt special. Good vibes waited for her on the island, but the emotion passing between her and Peter, this sweet tenderness, was all that mattered. "The weekend has started and I'm grateful to share it with you."

WHEN THEY ARRIVED at the dock, Peter helped Claire exit the boat. He passed her suitcase into her hands and then grabbed the other two. The weather promised a perfect day. The sun bright and high in the sky. A gentle breeze blowing warm against his skin as they walked across a planked wharf and climbed a flight of wooden stairs. After passing over a rocky slope with water beneath them, he escorted Claire to a simple white cabin with a wraparound porch. He pulled a key from his pocket while eyeing his beautiful wife. "Our home away from home…"

"What a cozy place," Claire said, moving toward the porch. She turned around and stared at the way they'd come, taking in a view of the sea. He looked at her, assessing her response, hoping she liked this beach house as much as him.

"The home has a southern exposure," Peter said. "Sunlight rises from the east in the morning and from the west at the end of the day."

Claire walked to the eastern side of the house. She pointed. "Look—there's a bench. A place where we can enjoy our morning coffee." She eyed him briefly. "What an incredible view. How did you find this place?" She loved the house. He could tell. Interest brightened her face.

A realtor had helped him locate the house, but it was too soon to tell Claire the truth. "I've been searching for weeks." He left their suitcases by the front door and joined her. "We've had a lot to overcome. Our anniversary weekend should be special. To celebrate a new life together. Do you want to see inside?"

"You say that as if you've already seen the interior."

"I might have." Peter grasped Claire's hand. "I had to prepare the cabin prior to our stay to ensure our needs were met. This is a remote location. We can't walk to the corner store if you have a craving." He'd satisfy her cravings...

Peter escorted Claire to the front of the house, sensing excitement in her cheerful expression. He placed the key in the lock and turned it, opening the door. "After you, my love." He gestured with his hand.

Claire passed by him, walking across the threshold. She paused on the other side of the doorjamb and studied the main room. Peter knew the room wasn't fancy, but the cabin offered the right amount of luxury. An alleyway of a kitchen with a rectangular counter. A table and four chairs in front of that. A comfortable sofa and a stone fireplace. A hearth and a home. What more did a couple need? Commitment and love.

But what did Claire think? Would she support the choices he had made with her, the work he had done alone? She walked to the table and fingered a wooden bowl filled with shells. He'd purchased the bowl, selected the shells from the cove, and placed the adornment on the table.

He asked the all-important question, "Do you like it, Claire?"

She gazed at him, a quizzical expression on her face. "The shells or the cabin?"

Peter left the suitcases by the door. "The cabin."

"It's more than I expected." She moved to the window and looked out. "It's private. It's quiet. And what an incredible view."

"What should we do now? Would you like to take a walk, go for a swim?"

Claire approached him and grasped his face, hugging him. "Thank you for this getaway. It means a lot to me."

"You're welcome," he said, breathing a sigh of relief. She liked the cabin. He kissed her.

"If you're not ready to see the ocean, I could show you the bedroom."

"I'd like that." She licked her lips, and the act fired his need. He couldn't look away from her pretty face.

Peter grasped her hand and led her to the back of the house. A simple room with a rustic bed and white sheets. A path of rose petals trailed across the bed. A towel made into the shape of a swan. A bottle of wine, chocolate strawberries held in a shell bowl on the dresser.

"How did you manage to add romance to this package?"

"Someone who lives on the island manages this property. I thought you'd like it. Do you?"

Claire grasped his face and pulled him closer, urging him toward the bed. He couldn't say no to his wife's desires.

"I love you, Peter."

CHAPTER TWENTY-SIX

Claire sat beside Peter on a wooden bench made for two. A rich landscape was in sight; trees, green foliage and an ocean that stole her breath. A painting couldn't do justice to this seascape.

"Thank you, Peter, for bringing me here."

"I knew you'd love it. You always said you wanted a place by the sea."

"Maybe we'll own a house near the water someday, but even a brief stay is better than none at all."

Yet Claire wished owning an ocean home was possible. Time had no meaning in paradise. She could wake at any hour. Read a book, listen to a podcast, or sit here watching the boats motoring across the strait. Peaceful...she sipped her wine, relaxed and calm, savoring the fruity mix that satisfied the palate. It tasted better while lounging on the deck, pondering a miraculous blue sea.

How had Peter found this place? She'd glance at him from time to time, wondering what he contemplated, worrying when this bubble might burst, but grateful too for his secretive planning that had brought her to this place. They'd only been on the island for little more than a day and she never wanted to leave. Never wanted to go back to Ocean Park or the responsibilities that lived there.

"Are you ready?" Peter asked, reaching for her hand.

"Yes, I think so," she said dreamily, studying him.

The setting sun lit his cheek bones, and she saw his handsome appeal. A few wrinkles creased the corners of his eyes, salt and pepper hair instead of a darker brown. When she studied him more intimately, he was still the boy she'd fallen in love with years ago.

Peter wouldn't have chosen such clothing then, a pale peach shirt and creamy pants. She'd never seen them before so they must be as new as her evening dress. They'd have to take a selfie of each other and send it to their kids. Neither of them had ever looked so good.

Claire searched Peter's expression, excited to celebrate their anniversary, and so much more.

He grinned, taking her hand, and urged her to rise from the bench. "You look stunning tonight. You're glowing."

"It's the dress. You have exquisite taste."

"No, it's not the clothing. It's you."

He gave her a slight smile as if to suggest his gift imparted something that happened every day, but the dress made her feel special. Made her feel loved. The chiffon fabric, a creamy confection with slender straps and a wispy skirt that fell to her feet. The fabric of a girl's dreams. She loved the way it felt, the way it swished and floated around her legs as she walked.

Peter had given her the best gift. Why had he chosen this dress? His newfound generosity pleased her.

Their fingers entwined together. A feeling of serenity passed between them. "Shall we begin our evening, Claire?"

"Yes, I'm ready."

"Come, let's go. We're dining in the cove."

Peter led her along the boardwalk on the east side of the cottage. They passed along a gorgeous twisting pathway, laden with foliage on either side. They walked among the greenery, holding each other's hands, meandering through this emerald forest. Trees with a carpet of moss coating their lower trunks. The forest floor a carpet of sword ferns, lily of the valley, and shrubs with tiny leaves.

"Does this pathway lead to the cove?"

Peter smiled at her. "I can't wait to show it to you. I hired a chef to cook a gourmet meal fit for a queen."

"You've thought of everything."

"I want you to have a special evening."

"It's beyond special. It's amazing. I can't believe we're celebrating twenty-six years of marriage. I'm worried if I blink, this magic we're creating together will slip away."

"I mean for it to last," he said, squeezing her hand. "Long after this night ends."

After a few minutes, they arrived at a picturesque cove. A table and chairs were placed on a rock patio, the table set with porcelain dinnerware. Though a chef and server were waiting, Claire didn't rush to take a seat. She paused at the base of the pathway, pondering the scenery. The private view left her speechless. As beautiful at the base of the hill as it had been from the top. The ocean rolled in and out. The air blew fresh and clean. "I love this, Peter."

"I knew you would."

She closed her eyes, breathing salty air, listening to the lull of the waves. A gentle swell, a slow current rolling across the sand, sweeping in and out, drawing her closer to the shoreline. A gorgeous table was set and waiting for them and all she wanted to do was search for shells.

Peter smiled as if he recognized her heart's desire. All this…because of him. She took a deep breath, trying to control the sudden emotion. Where did it rise from? This bliss, this joy in her heart was enough to make her cry.

"Good evening," the chef said. "Welcome to your anniversary weekend. We're ready to serve your dinner. Will you take a seat?"

Peter grasped her elbow. "Shall we, my love?"

Claire turned to him. "This is beautiful, Peter." She clutched his arm and he led her toward the table. There, he pulled out her chair and helped her to sit before taking his own seat. She glanced at him, the sea becoming a secondary view.

Their server, a young woman, came forward. "May I pour you a glass of wine?"

"Yes, please," Claire said.

"A little history around this wine, which your husband says is perfect for this evening's occasion. The Sea Star Ortega comes from the Clam Bay Vineyards on Pender Island. It has rich notes of peach, starfruit white, grapefruit and melon."

The server poured an ample serving into two glasses. Claire lifted hers and Peter lifted his.

"Happy anniversary, my love," Peter said, smiling. "Cheers to making more memories together."

They clinked glasses. Claire was suddenly overcome with emotion. She couldn't look away from Peter's face. The atmosphere and the man near her made the occasion memorable. *How did you thank someone for an occasion such as this?*

"I love you, Peter. I feel like a princess. Thank you for this weekend." Caught up in the emotions, she gazed at the sea momentarily. "This seaside vacation, it means so much to me. I'll never forget it."

"I hope that's true." He grinned at her, and she wondered what might come next.

The server brought them fresh bread. Claire broke off small pieces and dipped them in garlic-flavored butter. Peter took a sip of his wine, in no hurry to eat his bread. He studied her expression like a man desiring something more than food. "What's going on in that mind, Peter?"

"I'm contemplative, enjoying the moment, the wine, and the view."

"You're not even looking at the ocean."

"I'm looking at you." His comment made her speechless.

Listening to the breeze and the swell of the ocean, they were quiet as they ate. A fresh garden salad lightly covered with a citrusy vinaigrette. An entrée of seared scallops in a white wine sauce. Claire was full by the time dessert arrived, whatever it was, hidden beneath a large clam shell.

"Why don't we take a walk?" Claire suggested. "Watch the sunset, then return and have dessert."

Peter stretched forward, desire or some other intrigue

highlighting his expression. "Why don't we have a taste, see what we'll be coming back for."

Peter gave her an intent look. Claire reached for the clam shell and lifted the lid. And there inside, on a blanket of marzipan icing, was the most beautiful ring. It sparkled in the diminishing sunlight.

"Peter, what is this?"

Peter left his chair and kneeled near her. "I want this moment sealed with my love, more love than you've ever known. I want you to know that this new ring is an expression of my love and commitment to you. I'm prepared to do something I thought I'd never do."

Claire swallowed. "What's that?" she asked, whispering.

"Let's get married. Let's renew our vows. Will you marry me again?"

Emotion overwhelmed her in a good way. She joined him on the ground. "I don't know what to say."

"Honey, I'm on my knees. Say you'll marry me."

"Yes, I'll marry you." She hugged him. "Of course, I'll marry you."

They rose together and Peter removed the ring from its bed of icing. "This is a cultured pearl, it's circled with semi-precious diamonds."

"It's beautiful." Claire removed her wedding band from her ring finger and watched Peter slip the engagement ring on her finger, replacing their first commitment. "It's stunning. Beautiful. I adore the pink hue of the central pearl and the diamonds around the band are exquisite. I didn't expect this. You've completely surprised me."

"Our life together didn't begin in the right way, so this

moment is important to me. I want it to be perfect for you. You need to know that I don't regret one second of our life together. You are my rock. My world."

"I don't know what to say."

The sun dipped a little lower on the horizon.

"Before we watch the sunset, there's another gift I'd like to give you."

"Another gift?" Claire asked, staring at the ring. It felt strange having its weight on her finger.

"Yes, I want you to have it before there's not enough light to see."

"Okay." Her heart pounded. What could possibly top off an already perfect evening?

Peter pulled an envelope from his vest pocket and passed it to her. Was it an anniversary card? It must be something more. A wistful expression lit his face. He watched her as she opened the card, pulling out a postcard image of the vacation property they were staying at. The words had been notated simply. Peter wasn't a man of many words.

To my wife on our twenty-sixth anniversary,
You own a house by the sea.
With all my love, Peter.

Claire held the image in her hand. She stared at Peter, not sure what to say. She read the message a second time. *A house by sea…* "What does this mean?"

"I put in an offer on this seaside cottage. There's only one condition on the purchase."

Claire glanced at her ring, glanced upward at the cottage

built on the cliff's edge. "What is happening here? I don't understand. What are you saying?"

"I bought my beautiful wife a house by the ocean. The seaside home you've always wanted. A place to search for shells. A home to store them. Your very own sea for summer."

"With what money?"

But Peter didn't seem concerned about her surprise or her concern about purchasing this home. He laughed in response to her question, giving her a humorous look while taking a sip of wine.

"I sold my business."

"You what? Why!?"

"It was the right thing to do."

"Peter, please explain. I'm overwhelmed."

He grasped her hand and urged her to rise upward. "Let's talk about it while we watch the sunset."

Claire rose from the chair, and they walked a few steps toward the ocean. The color in the sky encouraged them forward. Incredibly beautiful, it blossomed with hues of orange and pink, and with the backdrop of a blue ocean, the view stole her breath.

This is mine, ours?

Claire thought about the highlights of the evening. A new ring on her finger, a cottage above the ocean, and the business Peter no longer owned. She turned to him, tears of happiness glistening in her eyes. She'd yet to receive the most surprising gift of all, the investment in the bakery, and knew how Peter had been able to make it happen.

He took her into his arms and held her. "What's wrong? Why do you weep? Doesn't this make you happy?"

"I'm in shock. We own a cottage?"

"Yes, if you want it. I want you to know that this second time around, this commitment I'm proposing, it's not about material things. I want *you* to know that I choose you. All of you. Every inch of you." His voice had more determination in it than she'd ever heard before.

Claire asked a commonsense question: "I appreciate the gesture. I really do, but we can't afford this place. It must be worth a pretty penny."

"Yes, we can. I did better than expected from the sale of my business."

"And we haven't talked about the sale. Why didn't you tell me? Shouldn't we discuss major life decisions?"

"Probably," he said quietly, massaging her fingers, "but it wouldn't have been as special."

"It was special. I'm grateful," Claire said.

"I don't want further space between us. It's a good thing you showed me how to make a pie, because honey, you have a new partner at the Old Thyme Bakery and Café."

Claire shook her head, giving him a half-smile. "I wondered when you'd get around to telling me." She should be annoyed that she'd been left out of the decisions, but the generosity of his actions filled her heart with gratitude.

"Congratulations and happy anniversary," The chef said. He gave each of them a glass of sparkling wine. Peter lifted his glass and Claire did as well. "To our future," Peter said, gazing into her eyes.

They clinked their wine glasses. "To our life together," Claire replied, having more love in her heart for this man than ever before.

CHAPTER TWENTY-SEVEN

*C*laire glowed with happiness on her wedding day. In the cottage on Ruxton island, in a vacation home she appreciated having as her own, Stephanie weaved her mother's hair, more silver highlights than blonde these days, into a messy bun.

Time had passed quickly. Claire couldn't believe the renewal ceremony was about to happen, and she was delighted that her children, family and friends, could share this special day with them.

"It's good to see you happy. I love your dress. You look beautiful, Mom."

Claire glanced at Stephanie while sitting in front of a vintage makeup dresser. "You're the beauty, but your compliment warms a mother's heart."

Stephanie stood behind her, a serious expression on her face while twisting layers of hair into place. "I want the best for you."

"I have the best. I have my daughter and my family with

me on my wedding day." Claire grasped Stephanie's hand. "I'm glad you're able to share this with your father and me. I know how busy you've been."

Claire released her hold and Stephanie dotted her face with peach blush. "Where else would I be, but with my mom and dad. It's summer. I have a break from school. And let's get real, now that Dad and you own the cottage, Chris and I will come home more often. You can't be here every weekend."

"I'll hold you to that promise. We barely see you as it is," Claire said. It would be great to see her adult kids more often. She wanted to share this cottage with her family. Peter did as well.

"How's Dad managing at the bakery?"

"He's okay, but I've never seen so much flour on his clothing," Claire said with a giggle.

The new memories they were creating at the Old Thyme Café caused her eyes to water. Peter gave this work a lot of effort. The renovations in the café portion would be complete soon.

"Your father's better suited to refurbishing the cottage, but he never complains and always digs in wherever he's needed."

"He's always been a generous man, even when he was busy. I still can't believe he sold the business." Steph paused. "Mom, your eyes are full of fluid. You can't cry. You'll spoil your makeup."

"I'm not worried about my makeup," Claire said, wiping away a tear. I'm grateful to have my family together. Grateful to have this second chance with your father."

"Dad hired a photographer. He wants to capture every moment. It's important to him."

Claire was aware of this. Peter had bought a camera for himself and had taken up photography. Pictures of bakery renovations. Images of gulls and great blue herons. And his wife when she let him capture her image.

"He's told me as much."

Like her mother, Stephanie became wistful. Claire studied her as she reached for a hairpiece adorned with pearls. She placed it in her hair. "The perfect complement for your updo. You're not a new bride, but you should feel like one. My gift for my mom on her special day."

Claire became wistful for a moment. Her eyes threatened to fill with tears again. "This means a lot to me. I'll wear it with pride."

"Maybe you'll wear it when I get married."

"Are you dating?"

"Not yet, but there might be someone special." Stephanie smiled, glancing at the floor. Claire was certain there was someone in her daughter's life.

"Chris and I are happy for you guys. We were worried, worried our parents might…"

"…divorce?" The look on her face pierced Claire's heart. She didn't want to worry their children. "This is a happy day. A day for new beginnings; new memories, like the pictures your father wants to capture. A time for joy, not sadness."

Stephanie stepped backward and reached for a mirror on the dresser. "I can't wait to celebrate with you. What do you think, Mom? Do you like it? Did I do a good job?"

Unsure how to respond, Claire grasped the hand mirror and perused her image in the glass. A middle-aged woman stared back at her, and she reflected on the creases at the corners of her eyes, lines at the bridge of her nose, and soft skin that was no longer supple. Still, her daughter had applied a long-wearing foundation, and with peach blush and nicely painted eyes, the look complemented her complexion. She might be older, but looked and felt beautiful.

"You're quiet, Mom."

Claire placed the mirror on the dresser. "It's great to have you home. You've made me feel special and loved. Thank you, Stephanie."

"You're beautiful, inside and out." Stephanie reached into her bag and retrieved a box tied with an ivory bow. "Dad wanted me to give you this."

"Really? Your father, he's been full of surprises lately."

"A girl appreciates being appreciated, if you know what I mean." Stephanie winked, passing her the box. "Open it, Mom. I'm dying to see what's inside."

Claire held the gift in her hands while studying her daughter, seeing a younger version of herself. Stephanie had chosen to wear a pale peach summer dress. The style complemented her mother's ivory gown, which contained a lace bodice with tiny seed pearls and Swarovski crystals. And with layers of chiffon, the dress was perfect for a walk across the sand.

"Come on, Mom. Dad will be waiting."

Claire slipped off the bow and opened the box. She gasped at the sight of a three-strand pearl bracelet with gorgeous crystal spacers. "Oh my," Claire said, sighing, "your father has exquisite taste."

"He said to tell you the pearls represent the memories he plans to share with you."

Claire took the bracelet out of the box and held it in her hands. If these pearls represented their life together, they had a long journey ahead of them. Tears glistened in her eyes as Stephanie undid the clasp and placed it on her wrist. "He's so thoughtful. So full of surprises."

"You love it, don't you, Mom?"

Claire admired the bracelet adorning her wrist. "Oh yes, it's absolutely stunning and perfect."

Stephanie glanced at her watch. "It's time to take your walk. Are you ready?"

Claire nodded, smiling. "More than ready."

Claire accepted the bridal bouquet of peach, blush, and white roses from Stephanie. They gave each other a hug at the doorway, neither of them speaking, then passed through the door and began their descent to the private cove, where the renewal wedding vows were soon to take place.

A SMALL CIRCLE of friends and family waited for the bride and her daughter, and the guests were not disappointed. When a trio of performers began to play; a violinist, a guitar player, and a harpist, Claire and Stephanie made their entrance. Peter studied his daughter, as beautiful as her mother, as they paraded down the hillside. Claire paused at the base while Stephanie strolled forward, all smiles, seemingly pleased with the occasion. When she reached the ceremony spot, carrying a bouquet of flowers that matched the color of her dress, she stood on his right.

And then the moment came that Peter had been waiting

for. Claire strolled forward, flowers in her hands, her dress flowing between her legs. The wind teased her hair as she passed along a white-washed boardwalk in the center of the cove. He sucked in his breath, his pulse racing. Was this beauty his wife? His love, his everything...the partner he planned to make many more memories with for the rest of his life?

He was a lucky man, and he knew it. Fortunate to stand at the altar of their love, waiting for her to join him.

Claire drifted closer, a pleasant smile on her face. She nodded to their son when she reached the ceremony circle, then grasped his hand. *Was her hand quivering?*

Caroline began the ceremony, a perfect choice, as she had been responsible, in part, for bringing them back together.

"Welcome to this beautiful cove, and to Peter and Claire's renewal of their wedding vows," Caroline said. "It gives me pleasure to witness this special occasion. When I began my couple's retreat at Daydream Island, I could not have predicted a better outcome to my work than Peter and Claire renewing their wedding vows."

Peter grinned, glancing at Claire. Her blissful expression, pretty face, her hair so artfully done. He squeezed her fingers. He took a deep breath. "Caroline, on behalf of Claire and myself, we wish to extend our gratitude, not only for conducting the ceremony, but also for replanting seeds of love in our life. We're grateful."

"We'll build more bridges together," Claire said with a nervous giggle. "We won't fail next time."

"Here, here," Burt called out, their family and friends chuckling at the comment.

"Peter and Claire Douglas, you have worked hard in the past weeks to heal heartbreak, restore relationship connections, and make stronger memories together. I wish you much love as you move forward in your life. Are you ready to renew your vows?"

"We are," Peter and Claire replied.

Peter faced Claire and grasped her hand. She stared at him in a serene yet frightened way. "We've got this," he whispered, squeezing her fingers.

"Peter and Claire, is it your intention to reaffirm your marriage vows?"

Peter stared at his beautiful wife. "It is." Her voice blended with his in perfect harmony.

"Peter, do you vow to love, honor and cherish your wife, in sickness and in health, for richer, for poorer, for better or worse, for as long as you both shall live?"

"I do," Peter said, unaware of anything else but Claire.

"Claire, do you vow to love, honor, and cherish your husband, in sickness and in health, for richer, for poorer, for better or worse, for as long as you both shall live?"

"I do," Claire replied, smiling. Her voice proclaimed her confidence.

"On your wedding day, you exchanged rings as a symbol of your love. Rings serve as a reminder of your wedding vows. You've chosen to give each other new rings as you enter into a new commitment to live in unity, love and happiness."

When Caroline motioned to their adult children, Stephanie passed her mother a gold band and their son, Chris, passed Peter an eternity ring circled with baby diamonds. It slipped from his fingers and fell to the ground.

He dropped to the ground, horrified about the missing ring. Claire joined him. "Don't worry, we'll find it."

How could she be so calm? He scoured the sand, his fingers sifting through the particles, hunting for the ring. "Does anyone have a metal detector?" he called out in panic. If he ruined this day…

"I found it!" Claire said, laughing. All smiles, she leaned toward him. "Don't worry. Nothing is spoiling our day."

Peter studied her. Flushed skin and sparkling eyes. "I want to kiss you."

"Right here, right now, while we're on our knees?"

Peter licked his lips. "Maybe we should finish the ceremony. Our friends are watching."

"Yes," Claire replied. "I'm ready."

They stood and the ceremony continued.

Peter grasped Claire's left hand, repeating Caroline's words. "Claire, I give you this ring, a symbol of my love and commitment to you." Peter then slid the band onto her ring finger. He heard a tentative sigh.

Claire grasped Peter's left hand, also repeating Caroline's words. "Peter, I give you this ring, a symbol of my love and commitment to you." Claire slid the gold band onto his ring finger. When the ring was in place, she gripped his fingers and held on tight.

"This moment brings me much happiness. Peter Douglas, you may kiss your bride."

"My first bride and last bride." Peter kissed Claire. The kiss wasn't long, but when their eyes met, and they saw the love shining in each expression, they couldn't seem to pull apart. Peter kissed her again. "Happy day," Peter said, kissing her a third time. "I'll love you for the rest of my life."

"I'll always love you," Claire replied, squeezing his fingers, "from this day forward and for as long as we both shall live."

They faced their friends and family. "I announce to you, Mr. and Mrs. Douglas."

Clapping accompanied by hoots and hollering enveloped the couple with celebratory love. Peter and Claire broke apart, but still held each other. They had a lot of living left to do.

The best was yet to come.

THANK you for reading *A Sea for Summer.* I hope you enjoyed Peter and Claire's love story, your honest opinion of their romance will support the author's writing career. Please rate or review this book on your favorite book site, review site, blog, or your own social media properties, and share your opinion with other readers. Thank you!

Don't miss the next book in the series!
A Mountain Leads Home
(Taylor & Sarah)
Visit the author's website to read an excerpt:
https://shelleykassian.com/book/a-mountain-leads-home/

AUTHOR'S NOTE

Peter and Claire's story resonates with me for many reasons. The premise came while walking along the shores of Maple Bay at my summer home on Vancouver Island. Initially, I wanted to pay tribute to friendship; and three writing friends who I retreat with each summer, and church friends I retreated with when I was younger.

Women from varying cultures and backgrounds not only retreated from the stresses of everyday life, but also participated in meditation and healing experiences. I've been touched by laying-on of hands, or reiki. It's an enlightening experience. The song by Shaina Noll, *How Could Anyone,* warms my heart to this day. Years ago…a group of forty or more women sang it at retreat. I recall women weeping, who found it difficult to embrace their inner and outer beauty. For this reason alone, I included the song and the healing experience in my novel.

♪♫ *How could anyone ever tell you, you're anything less than beautiful…*

My husband also impacted this story. I wouldn't have envisioned it without his gift, my own sea for summer.

A *Sea for Summer* is the first novel in the Places in the Heart series. Sarah's story is available on November 15, 2022. Watch for Anne, Laina and Portia's stories, coming soon.

NOTES

CHAPTER 5

1. Shaina Noll, *How Could Anyone*. (Songs for the Inner Child, 2002).

CONTACT SHELLEY KASSIAN

If you would like to learn more about Shelley or her novels, visit her website at shelleykassian.com. Here you can read excerpts from her books, linked reviews, blog posts, as well as discovering her professional affiliations and accreditation.

Shelley enjoys hearing from her readers. If you'd like to contact the author, please send her a message at: shelleykassian@gmail.com.

FOLLOW SHELLEY ON SOCIAL MEDIA

amazon.com/author/shelleykassian

bookbub.com/authors/shelley-kassian

goodreads.com/shelley_kassian

facebook.com/ShelleyKassian

instagram.com/shelleykassian

twitter.com/@shelleykassian

linkedin.com/in/shelleykassian

pinterest.com/shelleykassian

ABOUT SHELLEY KASSIAN

Bestselling author Shelley Kassian has been writing timeless love stories filled with romance or dark fantasy (romantasy) for more than twenty years, novels that include her recent true love story, *A Mountain Leads Home*. A history enthusiast, she's traveled far and wide to explore secret gardens and medieval castles, having an avid interest in the Tudor period. Her prose has been described as "near rhapsodic," "pitch perfect," and "stylishly straightforward, rarely relying on complex turns of phrase." Reviewers have said her narrative conveys "imaginative fantasy," "fascinating characters," and "refreshing romance."

Shelley's taken creative writing courses, holds board positions within professional associations, and retains a Professional Editing Certificate. Drawing on her expertise, she has mentored novice writers, but her passion comes alive while scribing her stories into novel-length fiction. Shelley shares her life with her husband, adores her adult children and two grand pups, and when not relaxing at her seaside cottage, lives in Calgary, Alberta, Canada.

Manufactured by Amazon.ca
Bolton, ON